WHISPERS

Laurel House Series
Book One
By M. L. Bullock

Whispers Never Die

In the shadowed heart of Laurel's gate,
Whispers rise as day grows late.
Echoes of a time long past,
Haunting tales that ever last.
Midnight Veil with secrets deep,
In the garden, spirits weep.
Grave-soakers tread on hallowed ground,
Where lost souls are forever bound.
Pettie hears, in flowers' bloom,
Whispers calling, sealing doom.
A house of memories, dark and old,
Holds mysteries yet to be told.
Beware the footsteps in the night,
For shadows hide, away from light.
In Bryan Bay, where legends grow,
The secrets of the Whispers flow.
A tale of love, and loss, and fear,
Of things unseen, yet ever near.
In the heart of darkness, truth will rise,
For in the silence, Whispers never die.
M. L. Bullock, 2023

Chapter One–Grant

The gravel crunched under the carriage wheels as we approached the sprawling estate. Rows of ancient oaks lined the driveway, their gnarled branches reaching out like welcoming arms, swaying gently in the breeze. Virginia, my dear wife, leaned forward, her eyes widening with wonder and delight.

"Is this truly where you grew up, Grant?" she whispered, her hand instinctively clutching my arm. I could sense the mix of excitement and apprehension in her voice.

"Yes," I replied, my throat feeling unexpectedly tight. "This is Laurel House."

As we rounded the final bend, the grand mansion came into full view. Time had weathered its once pristine white walls, but it still stood tall and majestic, a testament to the craftsmanship of yesteryears. The large bay windows gleamed in the afternoon sun, and the wrap-around porch, though in need of a fresh coat of paint, beckoned invitingly.

I felt a familiar tug in my chest, a blend of pride and nostalgia. Yet, beneath it all, there was an inexplicable sense of unease. Memories of laughter, of family gatherings, and of sunlit afternoons spent playing in the gardens flashed before me. But there was something else, a shadow lurking just beyond the edges of my recollection.

A whisper of a memory that I couldn't quite grasp.

Virginia's gasp pulled me from my reverie. "It's beautiful, Grant. Truly, it is," she exclaimed, her eyes taking in every detail of the mansion.

I smiled at her, squeezing her hand reassuringly. "It's been years since I last saw it. I had almost forgotten how grand it was, myself."

From the back of the carriage, I could hear Pettie and Alan's excited chatter. They pressed their faces against the window, their eyes sparkling with anticipation. To them, Laurel House was an adventure waiting to be explored, a vast playground filled with secrets.

At least the children were excited about this adventure.

As the carriage came to a halt, I stepped out, taking a deep breath. The scent of blooming roses and fresh-cut grass filled the air, but beneath it, there was another smell, faint but unmistakable—a mustiness that spoke of closed rooms and untold stories.

"We're home," I whispered to myself, trying to shake off the uneasy feeling. Had Laurel House ever felt like home to me?

Virginia joined me, her arm looping through mine. It was as if this wife of mine could read my mind. "It's going to be a fresh start for us, Grant," she said, her voice filled with hope. "We're leaving the old life behind. This is a new and shiny start, darling."

I nodded, looking up at the grand facade of Laurel House. "Yes," I agreed, "a new and shiny start."

Yet, as we made our way up the steps, that nagging sense of unease lingered, a silent whisper warning me that some chapters from the past are never truly closed.

The doors of Laurel House opened with a soft, mournful creak, revealing a grand foyer bathed in the golden hues of the setting sun. The high ceilings, ornate chandeliers, and dark wooden stairway hinted at the mansion's former glory. Dust particles danced in the beams of light, and the air felt heavy with years of silence. The place was relatively clean, I'd made sure of that before we arrived, but it still needed the touch of someone more efficient, like our Mrs. Higgins.

Virginia, taking in the vastness of our new home, let out a sigh of contentment. "It's even lovelier on the inside, Grant," she remarked, her fingers trailing over the polished banister. "With a little bit of work, this place will be as grand as any home in Baltimore."

I nodded, appreciating her effort to remain upbeat.

The journey from Baltimore had been long and tiresome. The city, with its bustling streets and towering buildings, felt like a world away. We had left behind friends, memories, and the life we had known. My dismissal from the law firm, following a case that had gone horribly wrong, had been the final push.

Laurel House was our chance at a fresh start, a place to rebuild and find our footing once more. It had been sitting empty for years since my father's passing. I'd never dreamed of returning, but we truly had no choice. Baltimore society had turned against us in a horrible fashion. One that I could never have imagined.

New and shiny start, Grant.

Alan and Pettie, bursting with youthful energy, were already eager to explore their new home. "Father," Alan began, his eyes wide with curiosity, "may we explore? I want to see everything!" My son's normally serious expression had vanished and for a moment, he was a child again. Alan had always been an old soul. I was happy to see his childish zeal return. Intelligent and perceptive, Alan, although only nine, understood what was being said about his father. What was being said about his family.

Pettie nodded in agreement, her tiny chubby hand clutching her brother's. "Please, Father? I promise we'll be careful. Even on the stairs." My daughter's round face and vivid blue eyes always charmed me. Virginia attributed those eyes and cheeks to me, but I saw my mother's face looking back at me.

She would have loved Pettie. Too bad she never met her.

I hesitated for a moment, the unfamiliar shadows of the mansion looming large. But seeing their eager faces, I relented. "Alright, children," I said with a smile, "but stay together, and don't venture too far."

The children cheered, their laughter echoing through the hallways as they began their adventure. Virginia, watching them with a fond smile, remarked, "They're going to make so many wonderful memories here."

I hoped she was right. But as we ventured deeper into the house, the weight of the past pressed down on me.

Every creaking floorboard, every whispering curtain, seemed to be trying to tell me something. Something I had unfortunately forgotten. It was as if the walls held secrets, waiting for the right moment to be revealed.

My back felt icy cold as if an invisible hand rubbed it. I shivered slightly as Virginia patted my shoulder to comfort me. "Catching a cold, dear?" I assured her I was not, but said nothing else.

We explored room after room, each space a testament to the grandeur of a bygone era. Built by my grandfather in 1830, there were many vintage pieces. All of which felt as if they belonged. How could we ever replace them? Even my stylish wife was enchanted by the antiques.

The drawing room drew her attention, with its grand fireplace and plush armchairs. Thankfully, the cleaning company had done a good job of dusting the cushions and polishing the wooden tables.

The dining hall with its long table set was for a feast that had not yet come, but we were here now. Home. Laurel House was home again. But it was the portrait hanging in the main hallway that stopped me in my tracks. It was an image of a young man, his features eerily similar to mine. The plaque beneath read, "Grant Sullivan Sr., Founder of Laurel House."

Surely, I had seen this before. I'd grown up here. Why couldn't I remember? Why didn't I recall seeing this?

Virginia, noticing my fixation, gently squeezed my hand. "Your grandfather?" she inquired.

I nodded slowly, my voice barely above a whisper. "Yes. I never met him, but Father used to speak of him often. He said I had his eyes."

We stood there for a moment, lost in thought, the weight of history pressing down on us. Virginia, ever the beacon of hope, broke the silence. "We're going to make this house a home again, Grant. For us and for future generations. And look, your grandfather approves. I swear, I do see a smile on his face."

I smiled, drawing her close. I saw no such smile, but I would not fault her for seeing what she wanted to see. "I know we will," I replied, trying to sound more confident than I felt. But deep down, the unease remained, a silent reminder that every new beginning comes with its own set of challenges.

Outside, the clouds had gathered, casting a gray pallor over the grounds.

The first droplets of rain began to fall, pattering gently against the window panes. As the rain intensified, Virginia and I turned our attention to the small contingent of servants who had accompanied us from Baltimore. Their carriages had finally arrived. The staff awaited instructions, their faces a mix of curiosity and apprehension.

"Mrs. Higgins," Virginia addressed our housekeeper, "please see to the bedrooms first. We're all quite tired from the journey and will need our rooms prepared. Yours as well. Supper should be light. Don't exert yourselves too much today. I can see that you're all tired."

The stout woman nodded, her efficient demeanor instantly putting me at ease. "Of course, ma'am. I'll ensure everything is in order."

"For those you can spare," I added, "please begin with unpacking the essentials. And Mr. Doyle," I said, addressing our butler, "ensure the kitchen is stocked and prepared as we requested. If there's anything missing, you'll have to make a trip to town in the morning."

The servants dispersed, each attending to their duties. The house, which had been silent for so long, was now filled with the sounds of life – footsteps echoing, doors opening and closing, and the distant hum of conversation.

It wasn't long before Alan and Pettie returned, their faces flushed with excitement. "Father, this house is enormous!" Alan exclaimed, his eyes shining. "And there are so many rooms to explore! It's like a castle with nooks and crannies. We could hide and you would never find us!
"

"Never find us!" My daughter repeated, her face damp with sweat. Pettie, clinging to a small porcelain doll she'd discovered, added, "And there's a lovely garden outside with the prettiest flowers! Can we go see it?"

I glanced outside, where the rain was now coming down in earnest. "It's raining quite heavily now, my dear," I replied gently. "But I promise, we'll explore the garden first thing tomorrow."

The promise of tomorrow's adventure seemed to placate the children. As evening approached, we gathered in the dining hall. A simple but hearty meal had been prepared – a stew, freshly baked bread, and a pitcher of cold milk for the children, wine for Virginia and me. The warm glow of the candles illuminated our faces, casting flickering shadows on the walls.

As we ate, the conversation turned to the future. "I've heard there's a lovely church in Bryan Bay," Virginia mused. "Perhaps we could attend the Sunday service?"

Alan, ever the adventurer, chimed in, "And maybe we could get a horse? I've always wanted to learn to ride, Father."

Pettie, her voice soft, added, "I'd like to plant more flowers in the garden. Pink ones and purple ones.

I smiled, listening to their hopes and dreams. "We'll do all of that and more," I assured them. "This is our new beginning, and we'll make the most of it."

The evening drew to a close, and one by one, we retired to our rooms. The comforting chatter of the dining hall faded as we ascended the grand staircase to our respective rooms. The house, which had felt lively just moments ago, seemed to shift as night settled in. The hallways, bathed in the muted glow of the wall sconces, took on an eerie quality. Every creak of the floorboards, every rustle of the curtains, seemed amplified in the stillness.

As I made my way to the master bedroom, I couldn't shake the feeling that I was being watched. More than once, I thought I saw shadows darting just beyond my line of sight.

The sounds of the house, which should have been familiar, felt foreign and unsettling. It was as if the very walls were whispering secrets, tales of times long gone.

Why can't I remember? What have I forgotten? I tugged at my tie in frustration and willed myself to push my apprehension to the side.

Once inside the sanctuary of my bedroom, I tried to shake off the unease. Virginia, sensing my disquiet, took my hand. "I can see it in your handsome face—you're unhappy, Grant. By why?"

I shook my head, unable to think how to answer her question.

"It's just the weight of the world," she whispered, trying to reassure me. "It is not yours to carry. Not anymore. The jury made their decision, not you. You did your best, as you always do."

"I know, I know," I said woodenly.

"Soon, this place will feel like home and you will forget all about rotten old Baltimore. We'll make our home in Bryan Bay a showplace. A world of our own. Laurel House, what a lovely name. It must be a lovely place, Grant."

I nodded, appreciating her effort to comfort me. "You're right," I murmured, pulling her close. "It is a lovely place. Pay no attention to me, dear. It's just been a long week."

As I lay down, sleep proved elusive. The patter of the rain against the windows and the distant rumble of thunder only heightened the uncomfortable atmosphere in the room. My wife snored lightly beside me. I didn't mind. She was such a lovely, sweet woman. A woman I didn't deserve. Not really.

My mind, instead of resting, began to drift back to my childhood days at Laurel House. Broken memories flickered through my mind. Yes, fragmented memories played out like vignettes.

At least I remembered laughter, the scent of my mother's perfume, the sound of my father's deep voice reading bedtime stories. But interspersed with these comforting memories were flashes of something darker. Hushed conversations I'd overheard, the anxious looks exchanged between my parents, and the nights when I was certain I'd heard whispers just beyond my door.

A particularly vivid dream took hold. Oh yes! I did remember that at least.

I had been a young boy, chasing after a lizard in the garden. He'd been a wily one, changing his color as easily as I blinked my eyes. I ventured further into the garden; my surroundings became unfamiliar.

The bright day turned to twilight, and the once cheerful garden transformed into a maze of towering hedges and thorny bushes. Lost and disoriented, I called for my parents, but my voice was swallowed by the dense fog that now enveloped me. Where had this come from?

Emerging from the mist, soft whispers grew in intensity, beckoning me towards an unseen force. *The whispers! How could I forget the whispers?*

I awoke with a start and I was drenched in sweat.

The first light of dawn was beginning to creep through the curtains, casting a soft glow over the room. The dream, though faded, left a lingering sense of dread. Virginia stirred beside me, her face etched with concern.

"Another nightmare?" she asked softly. "Would you like a cup of water?"

"No water." I ran my hand through my damp, sweaty hair. "Just a bad dream. Go back to sleep, Virginia."

She smiled up at me sweetly, it was a smile that stirred me but I did not seek her comforts. Instead I held her and I too managed to slip back to sleep.

My nap was all too short. My eyes were sticky and tired, but I couldn't delay my duties. I had a new life to build.

And it started today.

Chapter Two–Pettie

Sunshine sneaked in through the curtains, making my room all glowy and warm. I rubbed my eyes and looked around, feeling kind of lost for a second. During my restless sleep I'd forgotten that I was in my new home. My new room. Yes, this room was way bigger than my old one. And it felt different, like when you get a new dress and it is still a little itchy. You have to get used to new dresses, probably new rooms too.

I wriggled out of the twisted sheets and swung my feet over the side of the bed. My feet didn't even touch the ground. This bed was so big! It was like one of those princess beds I read about in my storybooks. This bed had pretty wooden pictures of birds and flowers on the wooden headboard, and there was a floaty, fairy curtain hanging above me.

The blanket was super soft, like Mother's hugs, and it was pink—the best color ever! Well except for blue. That was actually my favorite color. I hugged the blanket close, remembering how I'd felt all snug and cozy last night.

Maybe tonight I'd have dreamy adventures in this bed. Mother always said fairy tales happen when you dream. In that case, I'd dream of meeting the Froggy Who'd Gone A-Courting or perhaps Little Bo Peep.

This new bedroom might be fun after all.

Today, I wanted to wear my blue dress, the one with the little white flowers on it. Luckily for me, it had been unpacked already. I found it hanging in my closet, but it took me a while to get the buttons right, but I did it. All by myself. When I finished sweating over the buttons, I pulled on my white tights and put on my shiny black shoes.

My hair was all messy, like a bird's nest. Usually, Mother or one of the maids would comb my thick blonde hair and tie it back for me. But today was different; I wanted to do it myself. The house sounded very busy, and I didn't want to wait for someone to come. I was always last, and I had a garden to explore. It wasn't raining at all this morning.

I grabbed my big ribbon and tied it around my hair, just like Mother did. Kind of.

Suddenly, I heard fast steps coming toward me. It was Mrs. Higgins, Mother's maid. "Miss Pettie!" she called out, trying to catch up to me. "Your hair! And your dress! Let me help you, child. Your buttons are crooked, and your hair has not been properly brushed. If your mother saw you! I shudder to think what she'd say."

But I was too quick for her.

I giggled and ran past her easily. I headed out to the garden before she could catch me. Mrs. Higgins called my name again and again but I wouldn't slow down. After the jostling ride yesterday and the day before that and the day before that, I wanted to run. As fast and as far as my legs would carry me.

The lovely garden welcomed me. It smelled so nice, a sweet combination of cool, fresh flowers and morning dew. Who would blame me for wanting to run free here?

There was a special garden with lots and lots of pink and white flowers. Mostly pink. Mother told me that these big flowers were called peonies. They looked like big fluffy pillows, and I wanted to touch them all. I had never seen such flowers before and I was quite familiar with roses. Mother loved roses and loved growing them.

As I walked closer, I heard something... weird.

Voices! They sounded soft—they were whispers, soft and barely audible. At first, I thought the flowers were talking to each other, like in fairy stories. But the more I listened to the voices, the more they sounded like children. Many children!

I smiled at hearing their voices, but they remained elusive. I spun around, but I didn't see anyone. "Hello? Are you there?" I said curious about the invisible invaders to my garden. "Who's there? This is private property, you know." I wasn't actually sure what that meant but I'd heard Mrs. Higgins say it many times, at the old house and this one.

The whispers kept speaking, but they didn't answer my questions. I couldn't understand what they were saying at all. It felt like a game, like hide and seek only a cruel game.

Maybe the whispers wanted to play with me? "Hello? Hello? Where are you? I can't see you!"

The whispers drew closer. They felt like a soft, tickly breeze on my neck, making me turn around and around, trying to find where they came from. I peeked behind big flowers and looked up into the trees, but there was no one there. The garden was big and full of secret places, but I didn't see any children hiding.

But then, the whispers changed. It wasn't just children I heard speaking—I heard a woman! A woman who didn't like me. No, she didn't like me at all.

In fact, I was pretty sure I heard her say my name but with a lot of hatred. Why would the strange lady hate me?

I paused in the middle of the garden suddenly feeling the need to make water. Try as might, I couldn't move. My legs wouldn't budge from the spot. I was afraid—too afraid. Afraid of the horrible whispers.

Suddenly, I heard Mother calling me. "Pettie! Pettie, dear! Breakfast is ready!"

Hearing Mother's voice set me free. I ran from the whispers—back to the house, my shoes tapping on the stone pathway. The smell of warm bread and eggs filled the air as I stepped inside. Everyone was sitting at the big table, plates full of food in front of them.

Mother looked up as I entered, her eyes first filled with relief and then a hint of surprise. "Oh, Pettie," she said, her voice gentle but a little stern, "just look at you. Your dress is buttoned wrong, and that ribbon in your hair is nearly falling out." To my absolute joy, Mother laughed aloud and I breathed a sigh of relief.

Mrs. Higgins, rushed over, looking worried. "I'm so sorry, ma'am. I tried to catch her, but she ran from me before I could help her dress."

"Pettie," father pretended to scold me.

Mother smiled, her face softening. "It's alright, Mrs. Higgins. I'm proud that my little girl wants to be independent and dress herself. But, Pettie, remember, all young ladies need a bit of help getting ready for the day."

Feeling a little embarrassed, I nodded and took my seat, eager to dig into the warm breakfast and forget all about my mismatched buttons. As I climbed onto my chair, I remembered the whispers.

"Father," I began, my voice soft, "are there other children here at Laurel House? In the garden, maybe? I heard voices. A bunch of children and a lady."

Father looked up from his plate, his face serious. "No, Pettie," he said, his voice deep and calm. "There are no children here, only us."

"But I heard children," I insisted, looking down at my plate, feeling a little embarrassed.

Father's face looked worried, and he exchanged a glance with Mother. "You mustn't go to the garden alone. Not yet. Not until Mr. Boyd and I have a chance to search it. I guess there could be a lost child wandering around," he said gently, his eyes searching mine. "Promise me you'll listen to me."

I nodded, not really understanding why, but wanting to make Father happy. "Okay, Father. I will stay out of the garden. I hope the children aren't really lost."

It was a disturbing thought, so I put the phantom voices out of my mind. The rest of the day was full of playing and exploring inside the house. But as the afternoon sun began to disappear, my thoughts went back to the garden.

Yes, I'd seen Father and Mr. Boyd go out to search it but they returned and had not said a word. Father was in his study with the door closed, but I had to find out more about the strange voices. Why would the children hide from me? I was just another child, not someone they should be afraid of. Not at all.

As I tiptoed back to the garden entrance, I spotted a white cat with one blue eye and one green one. He made a fine figure, sitting by the peonies. *No, I wasn't going to go into the garden. Was he here to tell on me?* He looked at me with a bored expression, and I giggled.

"Hello, Mr. Cat. I guess you are a Mr. Are you a Mr. or a Mrs.? I can't tell, but I think you are a boy cat so you must be a mister. Will you walk in the garden with me? You won't tell on me, will you?"

The cat yawned as if he were bored at the very idea but he did indeed walk with me. For that at least, I was grateful.

I finally made a friend. Friends were difficult to make and even harder to keep. Even I knew that, and I was only six. I kicked a gravel rock and began to run, the cat kept up pace with me. I paused to laugh at him. He was such a pretty cat. All fluffy and friendly.

Hmm...I wonder if he'll let me pet him?

"I'll call you Leo," I said, bending down to pet him. Leo purred loudly as if he approved, rubbing his head against my hand. "Mr. Leo, if you prefer." Again, he yawned as if bored.

We played for a while, I was careful to stay close to the entrance of the garden. When it was time to go back home, Leo followed me, his tail waving high in the air.

I had a new friend, and I couldn't wait to introduce him to everyone. I found my brother easily enough. Alan was in the library, looking at a big map when I walked in. I didn't like books, not like Mother and Father. Not like Alan. Except picture books. I did like those, but those kinds of books were not easy to find.

The cat walked with me, his soft paws padding silently on the wooden floor. "Alan," I said, my voice quivering a little, "look who I found. His name is Mr. Leo." Alan was immediately surprised to see our new friend. I could tell by his big smile. "Isn't he a bundle of joy? I hope Mother lets me keep him."

"Maybe she will. It is a big house. Maybe we should keep Mr. Leo a secret. She can't make him leave if she doesn't know about him.

"But she will see him anyway and he's such a nice cat. Don't you think he's a bundle of joy?" I couldn't say where I heard such a description but it had certainly stuck with me.

"I don't know about that, Pettie," my brother pet the cat gingerly.

"Alan, I heard whispers in the garden. I think someone is hiding in there. Want to come help me look?"

Alan looked up at me, his blue eyes wide with surprise. "Again?" he asked. "You and your imagination, Pettie. It's just your mind, you know. Maybe there is a house nearby. You could be hearing noises from another house."

I felt a lump in my throat, but I tried to be brave. "I didn't see any house when we came here. Did you? And it's not a story," I said, my voice stronger. "It's really happening."

Mr. Leo jumped up onto the table, his curious eyes watching us. Alan reached out to stroke the cat's white fur. "Look at this smart fellow, Pettie," he answered with a pleasant smile. "Let's play with him before Mrs. Higgins discovers his presence. I think I like Leo better than Mr. Leo. What do you say, kitty?"

I got the hint. Alan didn't want to talk about the whispers in the garden. We played with Leo for a while, laughing as he chased after a ball of yarn. But after some time, Alan's face grew serious.

"You know," he began, "this house does feel...weird. I miss our old house even though this one is much finer."

I rubbed my nose, which felt a little damp. "What do you mean, Alan?"

Alan hesitated, looking around as if making sure no one else was listening. "It's just that some places in the house make me feel cold, even when it's warm outside." He rubbed his arms furiously as if to demonstrate how cold he actually was and I believed him.

I leaned in closer, eager to hear more. "Like where? Where do you get cold? In here? Are you afraid of our new house, Alan?"

Alan narrowed his eyes at me. "I'm not afraid of anything. You're just a little girl, Pettie. You wouldn't understand these things."

My cheeks grow hot with anger. "You're just a little boy, Alan!" I shouted, my voice echoing in the room. "I do understand! I am not dumb just because I'm a girl. What has mother told you about that?"

Without waiting for a reply, I turned and ran out of the library, tears streaming down my face. I could hear Alan calling me to come back, but I didn't stop. I ran all the way to my room, slamming the door behind me. I didn't care if Mrs. Higgins scolded me. At least Leo was right on my heels, meowing softly, trying to comfort me. He jumped on the bed beside me and stared at me with his strange eyes.

I buried my face in my fluffy pillow and allowed myself to cry. I let out all the frustration and sadness that suddenly weighed my heart down. Why wouldn't anyone believe me?

At least there were no whispers in my room. No invisible children taunting me. I blindly reached for Leo but my reaching hand found nothing. No fur, no Leo. I lifted my head and pushed my disastrous hair out of my face.

"Leo? Where are you boy?" Shoot. I meant to ask Grant if Leo was a boy. I forgot and he made me so mad. Imagine treating me like a child when he's a child too! I slid out of the bed and pulled back the quilt to search under the bed. "Leo?" He had to be here somewhere.

The cat wasn't under the bed at all. Nor was he in the closet or in my dresser and my bedroom door was still closed tight. I climbed back on my bed and drew my legs up around me. I didn't know what to do, to cry, to scream or go to sleep.

I was still there when Mrs. Higgins announced my bath. I was happy to leave my bedroom but was sad that Leo was missing.

I had to tell Alan. Once I wasn't made at him anymore. Tomorrow. I'll tell him tomorrow. I padded off with Mrs. Higgins and forgot my worries in a bubble bath.

Bubble baths usually cured everything but I couldn't stop thinking about Leo. As I sat in the warm water and played with the bubbles, I spotted the white cat watching me from the open door.

"Leo? Where did you go earlier? Did you sneak out of a hole? Is there a hole in my bedroom?" Rather than answer me, he licked his paw once and then trotted away. Just in time too.

Mrs. Higgins was on the warpath over something.

"Were you in the garden again, Pettie? You heard your father. Stay out of the garden, child." Mrs. Higgins waved my dirty shoes at me but she wasn't that upset. She just wanted me to know that she knew I'd been sneaking around the yard.

"Yes, ma'am," I answered her as I blew another batch of bubbles across the room.

I sunk beneath the water, my finger clenched my nose shut. I hated getting water in my nose. Mrs. Higgins didn't like it when I went under the water but I wasn't afraid of water. I knew how to swim. Mother and I used to swim in the pond together all the time.

I closed my eyes and counted to twenty. I took a deep breath and went under again. This time I counted to thirty. I was pretty sure I could count more but I wasn't good at counting. Not at all.

I stayed under a good long time and when I reemerged from the water, the door was closed and it was just Leo and I. He stared at me and I stared at him.

To my surprise, Leo blinked. It was a strange sight, a strange sight indeed. "Leo?"

And then suddenly I knew what Grant meant. I was cold, oh so cold.

All I could do was scream.

Chapter Three—Virginia

The Sunday morning sun cast long, golden rays across the town of Bryan Bay. The streets, lined with neatly trimmed hedges and white picket fences, gleamed brightly. Birds chirped merrily, creating a melodic backdrop to the sound of horse hooves clacking rhythmically on the cobblestone. I loved Sunday mornings. Always such a feeling of promise.

Grant and I, along with our children, made our way to the local church. Grant confessed that his parents had not been churchgoers, so he had no experience with the fellowship.

Yes, the air was filled with an undeniable sense of anticipation, of new beginnings. Grant looked rather dapper in his charcoal suit, his face a mask of stoic calm. But I could sense his underlying reluctance.

He'd never been one to embrace religious observance. Yet, he was here today for my sake. For our family. I was glad for that. For me, church had always been important.

From the harmonious hymns, the comforting words of the pastor, to the collective prayer of the congregation – they grounded me, providing a sense of normalcy amidst the chaos of life.

Especially after the ordeal we had faced in Baltimore. The whispered rumors, the accusatory glances, the pitying looks – they had become too much to bear. Imagine accusing Grant of throwing a case. Who ever heard of such a thing?

Pettie and Alan, hand in hand, walked beside us. They looked impeccable in their Sunday best. Alan, was every bit the perfect gentleman in his neatly pressed suit, and Pettie, radiant in her white lace dress. My heart swelled with pride looking at them. Such well-mannered, lovely children they were. Grant and I had been blessed to have such wonderful children.

The church, an imposing structure of stone and stained glass, invited me to explore it. Sunlight filtered through the windows created colorful patterns on the wooden pews, adding to the ethereal atmosphere.

As we took our seats, the choir began their rendition, their voices rising in perfect harmony, filling the room with a sense of divine presence. It was rather strange not to be greeted by anyone but every congregation was different. Perhaps the good folks of Bryan Bay were more reserved than my hometown of Baltimore.

The service was comforting and familiar. The pastor spoke of faith, of trust in the Almighty, of the assurance that He watches over each one of us.

I felt a tear escape, sliding down my cheek, as I thought of our recent trials. Were we being watched over? Had our move to Bryan Bay been preordained? I glanced at Grant, searching for answers, but his face remained impassive.

I, on the other hand, always found comfort in the hymns and sermons. They anchored me to a little piece of normalcy in the ever-changing world around us all. If I thought too much about how large the world was and how dangerous it could be, it took my breath away. Not because I was weak, I never thought of myself as weak, even if others did.

My sister Evelyn most assuredly considered me a weak, pitiful thing. A woman in need of a good marriage and a safe life. What was wrong with that? Why was a good, sensible marriage wrong? And what was so abhorrent about safety?

Evelyn the Great. The scholar, the independent woman. Right. Only she wasn't so independent after all. Was she? She too had married, only six months behind me, and unlike me, had not found domestic bliss. Before my mother passed like spring, Evelyn's situation as she put it, broke our mother's heart. Evely had always been so intelligent and practical. Too practical to give herself away before marriage. Right?

Evidently not. When Mother found out about my sister's trysts with her professor, she'd insisted that they marry. *Evelyn the Great had been brought down by her own desires.* I blushed at my own unkind thoughts. I didn't wish my sister ill. I just missed how close we used to be, before I realized she thought me beneath her.

I studied my husband, Grant, who on the other hand, loved me greatly. His attendance this morning was clear proof of our mutual love and respect. No, practicing religion had never been his strong suit, but he respected my wishes, especially after everything that had transpired in Baltimore.

Oh, that had been a horrible time. Simply horrible.

The things the papers wrote about him. The accusations were unbelievable. How could anyone believe that Grant Sullivan would intentionally lose? For what benefit? Certainly not his or ours.

Pettie only shifted around once or twice and Alan kept his eyes forward. But the light poured through the stained-glass windows, they drew my eyes to them. I had to restrain myself from gawking. I needed to set the example for my family.

At the end of the service, we rose to silently pray and I wiped away a tear from my eye with my gloved fingers.

Yes, the Lord had forgiven us. Forgiven us for whatever sins we had committed. We must have done something, right? I snuck another peek at Grant. *Had he prayed too? Had he asked for forgiveness? Did he need it? What if I didn't know the truth? Did I want to know?*

After the service, we were politely invited to a large meeting room where the other parishioners gathered for tea and light refreshments. I was excited to receive such an invitation. At first. As Grant went to speak with some of the men, I found myself amidst a group of elderly women, their voices low and full of whispers.

The women my own age appeared to distance themselves from me, despite my smiles and friendly waves. Pettie held my hand and I imagined I felt her shiver beside me. Alan had found another little boy and was chatting away with him.

Why were the younger women avoiding me? Had they heard the rumors about my husband all the way from Baltimore?

"Laurel House, you know, it's always had a history," one of the women said to me, her eyes darting around to make sure no one was eavesdropping. "Strange happenings, mysterious events. I've heard stories from my late mother about the grounds and those rituals."

Another woman nodded, her face pale. Their names escaped me. Had they even introduced themselves properly?

"Yes, that's true. Such rituals. It's said the Veil performed dark magic there. They removed all those grave markers, but the bodies...they're still there."

"The Veil?" I asked stupidly. *Grave markers? What were they talking about?*

I felt a chill run down my spine. This was the first I was hearing of any such stories related to our new home. We had come to Bryan Bay to start fresh, away from the whispers and scandal of Baltimore.

The last thing we needed was more gossip.

"The Midnight Veil! That was what they were called. Grave soakers. They were a powerful group, dark workers. There's been none more powerful than the Veil. Probably the most notorious group in the state and they practiced their magic on your property," the first woman informed me. Her yellow teeth put me off but I smiled and clutched Pettie's hand even more tightly.

What was the speaker's name again? Helen? Helene?

Out of the corner of my eye, I saw Grant making his way towards me. He must have sensed my discomfort. Truly I believed I might vomit. His tall figure emerged from the crowd, and he gently placed a hand on my shoulder, leaning in closer to whisper,

"Everything alright, Virginia?"

I looked up at him, my eyes filled with uncertainty. "Grant, are there graves on our property?" I asked in a whisper, forcing a smile for the sake of appearances. He did not answer but rather his face darkened.

How strange. Did he know about this? How could he keep this from me?

The room was abuzz with conversations, laughter, and the clinking of teacups. Yet, amidst the noise, one word seemed to stand out and echo in my ears—spiritualists. I strained to listen as a group of women, huddled in a corner, continued their hushed discussion.

"We should go, dear. Mrs. Higgins will have the afternoon meal prepared. Let's return home."

Grave soaking? What did that mean?

A shiver ran through me. The very phrase was both macabre and terrifying. Before I could process this further, a gentle hand tapped my arm. I turned to see a woman, slightly older than me, with a look of concern in her eyes.

"Mrs. Sullivan," she began hesitantly, "Be careful about letting your children play near the garden. There is strong energy there, strong and undeniable. Some admire places like the garden but I do not. Please, be careful!"

I nodded, thankful that someone at least sounded concerned about me and my family. "Thank you," I managed to whisper back but with no clue about what that might mean.

What was I expected to say about that?

"Excuse me, ma'am. Please do not fill my family's head with such stories. Honestly, I expected more from people of faith. Come, dear. It is time to go home," Grant sounded quite aggravated, but he wasn't rude. I wouldn't have fussed if he'd raised his voice. The minister gave us a look of concern, but he did not make his way to us.

My head swam as we walked to our carriage. As we made our way home, I voiced my concerns to Grant as quietly as possible. No need in alarming the children. "Do you think there's any truth to those stories?"

Grant squeezed my hand reassuringly. "Every old house has its strange tales, Virginia. That's not unusual. It's just idle gossip, wife. We will make our own happy memories at Laurel House. Pay the gossips no mind."

Pay them no mind? All I could do was stare at him.

When we returned home, I couldn't shake off the unsettling tales I'd heard about Laurel House. Every shadow, every creak of the ancient floorboards seemed amplified, turning my home into a chamber of whispered secrets. But I was determined not to let old wives' tales tarnish the beauty of our new beginning.

Walking through the grand hallway, I tried to focus on the majestic architecture, the intricate carvings, and the history that surrounded us. This house, with all its grandeur, was now ours.

A place for our family to grow, to laugh, to create memories. Yet, the unsettling stories kept creeping back into my mind, casting a shadow over my thoughts.

I approached one of the large windows that provided a clear view of the peony garden. The blooms looked serene, dancing gently with the breeze. But as I gazed out, my heart raced. The same garden that looked so peaceful was said to harbor secrets of rituals and whispers from the past.

Was it possible? Could such beauty hide a darker truth?

A soft knock on the door interrupted my thoughts. I turned to see Mrs. Higgins, holding a stack of fresh linens. "Ma'am, I brought the linens you requested," she said, her voice gentle.

Had I requested linens? "Thank you, Mrs. Higgins," I replied, trying to sound cheerful. "By the way, I know we haven't been here at Laurel House for very long but... Have you ever heard... stories about the house? About the garden?"

Mrs. Higgins hesitated, her eyes darting to the floor. "Well, ma'am, old houses like these always have tales attached to them. Some true, some just idle gossip. You know what that's like. People like wagging their tongues."

I pressed on, "But have you ever... experienced anything unusual here? You were here with the Sullivan family, with the first Mrs. Sullivan. Did she have...did she see anything unusual? What happened to her, Mrs. Higgins?""

She paused, choosing her words carefully. "What really happened to Mrs. Sullivan, I cannot say. Yes, I've been at the house twice now. Once when the old Mrs. Sullivan wanted to make Laurel House a showplace. She was a sweet woman, older than me but she was kind, and I was blessed to call her friend."

I had a hundred questions about my late mother-in-law but I hardly knew how to ask any of them.

Mrs. Higgins continued, "Now that you speak of, sometimes, when I'm working late, I think I hear sounds but it's an old house, ma'am. Old houses have their own language. We have to learn it."

I nodded, trying to take comfort in her words. "Thank you, Mrs. Higgins. Let's just focus on settling in."

The housekeeper gave a small smile, "Yes, ma'am. Best to keep our minds on the present. Let the ghosts of the past stay at rest. "

As she left the room, I took one last look at the garden, the sun casting long shadows across the blooms. I whispered a silent prayer, hoping that our days ahead would be filled with joy, free from the shadows of the past.

Later that evening, after the children had been put to bed, Grant and I sat in the study, the soft glow from the fireplace casting flickering shadows on the walls. I poured us both a glass of wine, the rich red liquid swirling in the crystal glasses.

Grant looked up from the papers he was reviewing and noticed the troubled expression on my face. "Virginia, you've been distant ever since we returned from church. What's on your mind?"

I took a deep breath, choosing my words carefully. "Grant, the stories I heard today about our home, about the peony garden...they've left me feeling quite unsettled. The Midnight Veil. It's not just the tales themselves, but the way people spoke of them—as if they truly believed them. Your family—surely you would have heard these stories before."

He set his papers aside, giving me his full attention. "Virginia, when I left Laurel House, I was but a boy. I've never head of the group. You'd be surprised at how much I do not remember." I wasn't sure I could believe him. He saw my expression. "It's true! It surprises me as well. I don't know why I can't rmember. Maybe I'm just getting old."

"You're not old, Mr. Sullivan," Mrs. Higgins announced as she brought our evening sherry.

"Every old property comes with its own set of tales. Some might be based on truth, but most are just fabrications or exaggerations. My father wasn't one to put in with such stories and my mother, well, like you, she was a woman of faith." His compliment did not go unnoticed. I smiled at him as I handed him his glass.

"But what if there's even a shred of truth to them?" I asked, my voice trembling. "What if the garden really was a site for those dark rituals? What is grave soaking, Grant? It sounds wicked. The children play there, Grant!"

Grant took my hand, his grip firm and reassuring. "Listen, love. We've only just moved in. Let's not let unfounded rumors taint our view of this place. I promise, if there's any truth to these stories, we'll get to the bottom of it. For now, let's not jump to conclusions."

I nodded, taking a sip of my wine. "You're right. It's just... I can't help but worry for the children. We can't expect Pettie to stay out of the garden for the rest of her life."

"We continue to search for where the noise is coming from. Have some patience, Mrs. Sullivan. Trust me, okay?"

I kissed his cheek. "I will trust you, Grant."

The night deepened, and the house settled around us with its familiar creaks and groans. We spent the next few hours discussing our plans, the renovations we wanted to make to the house, and our hopes for the children's education in Bryan Bay.

As the clock chimed midnight, we decided to retire to our bedroom.

Walking through the dimly lit hallways, I couldn't help but feel a sense of unease. Every shadow seemed to hide a secret; every whisper of the wind sounded like a distant voice. But I shook off the feeling, reminding myself of Grant's words.

Climbing into our grand bed, with its soft sheets and plush pillows, I nestled close to Grant, seeking comfort in his warmth. I secretly hoped he would pull me close to him, make demands of my body, but he did not. I could not understand why. I pinched my cheeks every morning and wore a touch of rouge on my lips but not enough to appear vulgar. Grant used to compliment my red lips and once upon a time, he couldn't stop kissing them.

But we had two children now and Grant had almost lost his business—and apparently, had lost interest in me. A lot had happened, but we were here together. As I drifted off to sleep, I hoped that the new day would bring clarity and peace.

I tossed and turned through the night but managed to garner a few hours of sleep. Presumably more than Grant as he was not in bed the many times I woke, and I was too tired, and disturbed to go search for him in the dark house.

The next morning, after the children had been fed and Grant had retired to his study for some quiet reading, I found myself drawn to the writing desk in the corner of the drawing room. The polished mahogany gleamed under the morning light streaming through the tall windows, and the sight of the inkwell and quill stirred something within me.

Sitting down, I pulled out a fresh sheet of cream-colored parchment and began to write.

"Dearest Evelyn," the ink flowed smoothly as my thoughts translated onto paper. Who else would I write? I had few friends left. Although Evelyn and I weren't close anymore, I considered her an intelligent woman and she was my sister after all.

She would help me find answers, surely.

The act of writing always had a calming effect on me. Perhaps once I got all my words on paper, I wouldn't even send the letter. I couldn't be sure.

Writing was a way to organize my thoughts, to put into words the whirlwind of emotions that often threatened to overwhelm me. And writing to Evelyn, despite our differences, felt like confiding in an old friend.

Yes, once we'd been friendly.

"I hope this letter finds you well. It's been a few days since we moved into Laurel House, and I must admit, the adjustment has been both exciting and unnerving," I penned down, detailing the events of our first few days—the church service, the rumors about the house, and Grant's reassurances.

"Midnight Veil. Have you ever heard such a name? As much as I want to dismiss the stories as mere gossip, I can't help but feel a sense of unease. The house, grand as it is, seems strange in its... I don't even know how to describe it. And the peony garden, with its intoxicating beauty, holds an air of mystery that both fascinates and terrifies me."

I paused, taking a moment to gather my thoughts. "I fear I will never convince Grant to return to church. Sister, I can't shake the feeling that there's more to these stories than meets the eye. What do you know about such things? Please inform me so that I may be reassured." Finishing the letter, I hastily expressed my desire to see Evelyn soon and how much I missed our conversations.

Sealing the envelope, I felt a weight lift off my shoulders. It was as if, by sharing my worries with someone else, they had become a little more bearable.

I decided to send the letter off later that afternoon.

For now, I placed it on the writing desk, feeling a sense of accomplishment. Writing had always been my refuge, a way to escape, if only for a moment, from the challenges of the world outside.

As the sun began its descent, casting a warm golden hue across the landscape, the sounds of laughter and chattering filled the dining hall of Laurel House. The large wooden table, ornately carved and set with fine china and silverware, was laden with tasty dishes.

Mrs. Higgins was good at her job and always prepared a roasted meat, fresh vegetables, and a delightful dessert.

Pettie, her eyes bright and animated, regaled us with tales of her adventures with Leo, the cat. "He's so funny, Mother! He tried to chase his own tail today and went round and round till he got dizzy and plopped right on the floor!" she exclaimed; her giggles, infectious. Always the storyteller, I couldn't be sure that Leo was a real cat. I hadn't seen one yet.

"But sometimes, Leo acts strange." She said as she scooped a spoon full of rice.

"Strange how, darling?" I asked curiously.

"Leo blinks when he's thinking really hard. And he knows all the secret spots because he disappears from my room and I didn't even open the door."

Alan, ever the storyteller, shared about the children he'd met at church. I could see that Pettie was a bit put out that Alan had taken over the conversation.

Unaware of my bad experience with the older women, Alan expressed his desire to return to cultivate his new friendships. "There's a boy, Tommy is his name, who says he can climb the tallest tree in Bryan Bay! And another, Amelie, who knows all the best places to find wild berries. They invited me to play!" His excitement was palpable, a sign that he was beginning to feel at home in this new place. "Can we meet and go see them soon? They are children of the minister. They live in the house behind the church."

I couldn't help but smile, watching my son's excitement about making friends. It was a comforting balm to the unease that had settled within me. I made a vague promise that we would go see them but I wasn't sure if I would fulfill his wishes yet. Maybe if I met the adults privately one more time, I would feel more confident about allowing my children to befriend theirs.

Grant, noticing my improved mood, raised his glass in a toast. "To new beginnings and the memories we'll create here," he declared, his voice warm and filled with hope. The clinking of our glasses resonated in the room, a symbol of our unity as a family.

As we continued our meal, Grant, with a twinkle in his eye, made a suggestion. "What do you say, Virginia, about hosting a small gathering here? Perhaps next weekend? It might be a good way to get to know our neighbors better and put to rest any lingering rumors about Laurel House."

The idea was enticing. I assumed he meant for me to invite people outside the gossipy church group. This would be a chance to make a positive impression on the townsfolk and perhaps, in the process, dispel some of my own apprehensions.

"That sounds wonderful, darling," I replied, warmed by Grant's thoughtfulness. "A fresh start for all of us. Mrs. Higgins and I will begin planning the party tomorrow."

The evening wore on, filled with more stories, laughter, and the comforting presence of family. With dinner concluded and the children tucked into their beds, Grant and I retreated to our chamber.

It was the largest bedroom in Laurel House, adorned with heavy draperies and antique furniture passed down through the generations.

The room had an air of regality, yet there was a coziness to it, a stark contrast to the vastness of the house itself.

I took a moment to pen a few lines in my diary, capturing the essence of the day, before extinguishing the desk lamp and joining Grant in bed. He lay there, his deep breaths indicating he was on the brink of sleep, the day's exhaustion taking its toll.

Again, he did not seek comfort in my arms. What was he waiting for? Couldn't he see how lonely I was for him?

The room was dimly lit by the flickering candle on the bedside table, casting dancing shadows on the walls. The silence was palpable, broken only by the occasional creak of the old wooden floorboards and the distant hoot of an owl.

As I lay there, trying to succumb to the embrace of sleep, a sound reached my ears. Footsteps. Soft, but deliberate, echoing down the hallway. Pettie? Was she out of bed? Was it the cat? No, it sounded like a person. An adult person.

My heart began to race. Grant remained undisturbed, his steady breathing a testament to his deep slumber.

I strained my ears, trying to determine the source of the noise. Was it one of the children? A servant perhaps? But the footsteps seemed... out of place, as if they didn't belong to the living occupants of the house.

Clutching the sheets tightly, I tried to rationalize the sound. It had been a long day—an even longer week—filled with a myriad of emotions. Perhaps my mind was playing tricks on me, conjuring up sounds borne from the day's unsettling tales.

Yet, as the minutes ticked by, the footsteps seemed to grow louder, closer. I felt an icy chill run down my spine, my entire being alert to the unknown presence. The temptation to cry out, to shake Grant awake, battled with the primal fear gripping me.

And then, as suddenly as they had begun, the footsteps ceased.

An oppressive silence descended upon the room, the only sound being the rhythmic beating of my own heart. With bated breath, I waited, hoping that the night would pass without further incident.

As the candle's flame slowly dwindled, casting the room into darkness, I closed my eyes, and descended into a dreamless sleep.

Chapter Four—Grant

The morning light painted the world in hues of gold and amber, casting long, eerie shadows across the sprawling grounds of Laurel House. I found myself irresistibly drawn towards the peony garden - a lush sea of crimson and pink blooms that swayed gently in the breeze.

It was this very garden that had ensnared Pettie's young heart with its mysterious allure, and now even Virginia, with her pragmatic demeanor, had expressed her concerns. To add to the enigma, Alan, ever the rational child, began to claim he, too, heard the faint elusive whispers amidst the petals.

The stone pathway, worn by time and overgrown in patches by creeping moss, crunched beneath my boots. Birds sang in the distance, but their melodies were overshadowed by the weight of my thoughts. Why had I allowed Virginia to coax me into attending the Sunday service at Bryan Bay's Methodist Church? We had never been particularly devout, and I questioned our connection to that specific denomination.

The whispers—those confounding murmurs that both Pettie and Alan spoke of—gnawed at the edges of my reason. Were these tales woven from the innocent fabric of childhood fantasy? Or was there, lurking in the shadows of our new home, a grain of unsettling truth? The garden, with its intoxicating fragrance and mesmerizing beauty, seemed to hold secrets just beyond my grasp.

As I neared the garden, the peonies burst into view, their petals a riot of pinks and reds, shimmering and swaying as if performing a waltz under the sun's gentle caress.

Amidst this floral spectacle, a familiar silhouette was hunched over, hands buried deep in the earth, carefully nurturing the blooms with the expertise of seasoned hands. The sun cast a dappled pattern on his worn hat, but even from this distance, I recognized the stature and the meticulous manner with which he attended to each plant.

It was unmistakably Quincy, the old gardener and my old friend. Yes, we'd been friends once upon a time.

Taking a deep breath, I called out, "Quincy?" My voice, hesitant at first, cut through the morning's serene stillness.

He rose, each movement deliberate and unhurried, the passage of time evident in the slight stoop of his shoulders and the creases etched deeply into his sun-worn hands. As he turned, his eyes, clouded slightly by age, sparkled with a flicker of recognition. A slow, genuine smile spread across his weathered face, revealing lines of countless smiles past. "Ah, Master Grant," he greeted, his voice a gravelly timbre softened by warmth. "It feels like lifetimes ago since we last met. Welcome back to Laurel House."

Seeing him standing amidst the garden, memories cascaded back. As a young boy, my days were often punctuated by hours spent with Quincy. He'd weave tales about the flora around us, each plant carrying a story, a myth, a legend.

Under the vast sky, amidst the symphony of nature, he had been more than just a gardener to me – he was a mentor, a confidant, a beacon of wisdom. Yet, as the sands of time slipped away, those cherished moments had dimmed, stored in the dusty corners of my recollections.

The moment our eyes met, a tidal wave of memories surged forth, recalling days of youth when I'd chase butterflies across these very gardens, with Quincy's laughter echoing in the distance. The weight of the years bore down heavily between us, bridging the gap of time with a silence that spoke volumes.

"Quincy," I began, my voice thick with emotion, "Seeing you here... it's like stepping back into a dream." I reached out offering my hand, not as the young boy he once knew, but as a man now weathered by life's trials. "And please, just call me Grant. I am no Master."

He grasped my hand, the rough texture of his palms a testament to the years he'd dedicated to this land. "Grant," he repeated, a hint of sadness in his eyes. "Time has surely flown. I remember when you were but knee-high, running through these gardens with your father and mother trailing behind."

A pang of nostalgia hit me. "Those days with you and my family... they were simpler times. Before the weight of the world pressed down upon our shoulders."

Quincy sighed deeply, his gaze drifting over the blossoming peonies. "Indeed. But this place, as beautiful as it seems, holds secrets. Secrets your father was aware of but chose to turn away from. I'm afraid it will fall on you now. Laurel House has become your burden."

A shiver ran down my spine, his words echoing the unease I'd felt since our return. "Quincy, what are you hinting at?"

He looked at me, his eyes searching mine, as if weighing how much to reveal. "This estate, its very foundations... are built upon things older than any of us. Your father knew, and his father before him, yet he remained silent. And now, with you and your family here, my concerns have deepened."

Tears brimmed in Quincy's eyes, the weight of decades of secrets pressing heavily upon his shoulders. "We can't erase the past, Grant. But some things refuse to be buried."

The sun hung lower in the sky, casting a golden hue upon the garden, yet its beauty was now marred by the haunting truths Quincy shared. The vibrant peonies, swaying gently with the breeze, now seemed like silent witnesses to forgotten tales.

I felt a cold shiver run down my spine, memories of my childhood playing in this very garden now tainted with a newfound knowledge. "My children," I whispered, the realization hitting me. "They've been playing atop... graves?"

Quincy nodded slowly, his gaze never leaving mine. "The whispers your children hear, they are the voices of those long passed. Spirits disturbed and restless. They were summoned, called forth from the darkness and they cannot rest. And the ones that called them, they will return too."

I stumbled back, my mind racing. The laughter of Pettie and Alan echoed in my ears, juxtaposed with the grim reality of the garden's past. "My mother," I choked out, the question burning in my throat, "did she know? Was her death... connected to this garden?"

Quincy's face grew somber, his eyes misting over with pain. "Your mother was a beautiful soul, Grant. She loved this place; she loved you with all her might. But she came too close to the truth. And some truths—or rather the revealing of—they come at a cost."

The morning air was thick with nostalgia as I stood beside Quincy, the memories of our shared past echoing like whispers on the wind. Each blooming flower, each rustling leaf seemed to stir forgotten moments from the depths of my consciousness.

"Quincy," I began, the weight of years and unspoken words pressing down on me, "when I was a child, before I was sent away, we were friends, weren't we? You were my friend, Quincy."

His seasoned eyes met mine, glimmering with a mixture of warmth and sorrow. "Yes, Grant. You were like a son to me in many ways. After your mother's passing, you'd find solace in the garden, with the plants, with me. We'd spend hours talking, not just about the flowers, but about life, dreams, and all that lay between."

My heart ached with the sudden rush of memories, of days filled with innocent wonder and nights haunted by loss. I felt afraid of Quincy, but I also experienced a strange sort of hurt, as if he'd abandoned me. Had he?

"But why did you leave, Quincy? After my mother... after everything... and why did my father let you go?"

He looked down, his fingers brushing over a delicate peony petal. "Your father had his reasons, Grant. After your mother's death, there was a rift, a divide that grew between us. He believed in protecting you, in shielding you from the painful memories of this place, and perhaps from the truths he wasn't ready to face."

I felt a pang of anger, mixed with a longing to understand. "And what are those truths, Quincy? You keep hinting at it, but you haven't told me much."

Quincy's gaze was distant, filled with a profound sadness. "If I told you everything now, you wouldn't be able to process it. In fact, you wouldn't believe me, but I'll be here. I will be close. You'll have to wait, Grant. If you need me, come to the garden."

I laughed nervously. "Are you proposing I hire you as a gardener?"

"No, I'm not advocating for a job, Grant. I only want to be your friend. That's all I ever wanted."

A chill ran down my spine. The whispers, the memories, the unsettling feeling that had plagued me since our return; these were all related.

One thing I did know, my family was in danger, and I had unwittingly brought them into the heart of my childhood's high strangeness.

Lost in thought, I paused to take in the garden's beauty. The vibrant peonies, bathed in the soft afternoon sunlight, seemed almost surreal. The whispers of my childhood, the laughs, the joy, all seemed to echo faintly in the wind. But now, there was a shadow, a sense of foreboding that tainted those once cherished memories.

Quincy, perceiving my internal conflict, delicately reached into the pocket of his worn coat. From it, he produced a pendant, its surface slightly tarnished by time.

"This belonged to your mother," he murmured, holding it out to me. "She entrusted it to me for safekeeping. I believe it's time you had it."

The pendant was immediately familiar. A rush of memories flooded back, each one of my mother wearing the necklace and pendant, its silver surface catching the light. It was a piece of her, a tangible connection to a time before the pain, before the loss.

Holding it now, its cool metal warming in my grip, was both comforting and heart-wrenching.

Virginia's voice echoed from the garden's entrance, breaking my reverie. "Grant? Grant, where are you?" The urgency in her voice brought me back to the present, to the very real dangers that might be lurking in the shadows of our new home.

I pocketed the pendant, its weight a constant reminder of what was at stake. Turning to Quincy, I implored, "Promise me, Quincy. Promise you'll help us. Whatever's happening here, whatever the danger... We need you."

His eyes, filled with age-old wisdom and sorrow, met mine. "I've always been here, Grant. I'll do whatever I can to protect your family. You have my word."

With renewed determination, I headed towards Virginia, her silhouette framed by the setting sun. But just before reaching her, I cast one final glance back at the garden, at the spot where Quincy had stood.

To my astonishment, he was gone, vanished as if he'd never been there at all.

The realization hit me like a cold gust of wind.

Had I been speaking to a ghost?

I began to jog to the house. I longed for Virignia's warm skin and loving arms. I needed to feel a real woman, be in the real world.

Living among regrets and shadows, ghosts and tragedy, it wasn't a place I wanted to be. Tonight, I would lose myself in Virignia's embrace. Hopefully, she would welcome me.

I need you, Virginia. Need you to keep me sane. I thought this as I hugged her tight. Together we went inside and searched for our children.

Chapter Five—Virginia

Mornings at Laurel House unfurled with its customary symphony: the muted conversations of the house staff from distant corridors, the melodic chirping of birds heralding a new day, and the comforting cadence of household chores.

Grant expected me to plan a party but I wasn't excited about that, I couldn't say why. I was normally one to love parties and making new friends. But today, I wanted to get lost in my music.

Within the opulence of the drawing room, I settled myself before the grand piano, its glossy surface reflecting the room's grandeur. My fingers, once so adept, now hovered hesitantly above the ivory keys.

As I began to play, the familiar strains of a tune I'd learned as a young girl filled the room. But the music was punctuated with discordant notes, my fingers protesting with a stiffness and soreness born from years of neglect. Each faltering note was a cruel reminder of the many things I'd set aside, of passions forgotten in the whirlwind of life's responsibilities.

Pausing, I let out a sigh, allowing my gaze to wander to the window. I found myself yearning for the sight of the postman, hoping he'd carry a letter from my sister. Her writings were like a balm to my soul, threads of connection that bridged the distance between us. But the pathway outside lay undisturbed, devoid of any visitors.

The absence of her letter, especially amidst the disconcerting mysteries of our new home, felt like yet another note out of tune in the melody of my life.

The fluttering blur of azure caught my peripheral vision—it was Pettie, donning her cherished blue dress, as she spiritedly made her way toward the garden's embrace.

"Pettie!"

Time and time again, I'd cautioned her about the boundaries, imploring her to remain within the safety of the house's vicinity. Yet, the garden, with its intoxicating blend of colors and scents, appeared to beckon her with an irresistible pull.

"Pettie!" My voice rang out, an undercurrent of anxiety tinging each syllable, but it seemed to dissolve, unheard, in the vast expanse of the grounds.

Without a second thought, I found myself dashing after her, each heartbeat resonating in my ears like a frenzied drum. The click-clack of my heels against the cobblestone pathway seemed amplified, a stark contrast to the eerie silence that enveloped the garden. What usually felt like a sanctuary of flora, now seemed to transform into a labyrinth of shadows and uncertainty.

The towering trees and thickets seemed to whisper secrets, hiding my precious Pettie from view. "Pettie!" My voice wavered between hope and despair, slicing through the still air, desperately seeking a response. But all that returned was the haunting hush of the garden, amplifying my growing fear.

"Mrs. Higgins! Help me find her!" My voice, thick with urgency, broke through the stillness, echoing off the stone walls of the house. Every ticking second elongated, warping time, making each minute stretch out agonizingly. The vast estate, which once felt like a peaceful haven, now seemed a daunting expanse, hiding my dear Pettie within its secretive folds.

Mrs. Higgins, her apron fluttering, hurried out to help me, her usual composed demeanor replaced by palpable worry. The two of us, like frantic birds, darted to and fro, our calls for Pettie merging with the rustling of the leaves and the distant murmur of the waves.

The entire household soon stirred into action. The maids and even the kitchen staff abandoned their chores, spreading out, their voices joining the chorus of our desperate search.

Grant's normally steadfast face was now a canvas of deepening concern. Every wrinkle, every furrow, seemed to deepen with the weight of our shared anxiety. Alan, whose laughter I had heard earlier as he played with the cat, now stood, his youthful exuberance replaced by a look of mature determination, ready to join the search.

As the day wore on, the once golden sun began its descent, casting long, haunting shadows across the grounds. Its dwindling light painted the world in shades of orange and purple, and with it, a chilling blanket of desperation settled upon us all.

Each passing moment, with Pettie still missing, threatened to suffocate us in a grip of dread, tightening around our hearts.

As the inky blackness of night settled over the estate, it swallowed the once familiar contours of our home, transforming it into a vast, unknowable expanse.

Our lanterns, flickering like hesitant stars, pierced through the dense shroud, casting tall, wavering shadows that danced and played upon the landscape. Each rustle of the leaves, every creak of a branch, sent my heart racing, hoping against hope that it was a sign of Pettie.

The cold air clung to me, seeping through the fabric of my dress, chilling me to the bone. But it wasn't just the temperature that made me shiver; it was the harrowing thought of my precious girl alone, scared, and lost in this vast, shadowy world. The soft glow of the lanterns illuminated the anxious faces of our search party, their expressions mirroring my own deepening despair.

The rhythmic chorus of crickets, which on any other night would have been a comforting lullaby, now seemed to mock our efforts, their song intertwining with the echo of our desperate calls. I clutched my shawl tighter around my shoulders, but no fabric could shield me from the piercing cold of fear.

Every moment that Pettie remained missing felt like an eternity, and with each passing second, a heavy stone of dread lodged itself further in the pit of my stomach, threatening to pull me into an abyss of despair.

As the situation grew more dire, Grant's unwavering sense of duty took the forefront. With determined strides and a voice that held an edge of urgency, he reached out to the local authorities.

To our surprise and relief, the news of Pettie's disappearance spread like wildfire, drawing our neighbors out of their homes. Though our interactions had been few, the community of Bryan Bay rallied around us in our hour of need. Men with lanterns, women with shawls wrapped tightly against the chill, and even some older children, all came together, their expressions a mirror of our anguish, but also carrying a glimmer of hope.

Amidst the sea of concerned faces, a lone figure stood out.

A tall, thin man stepped forth from the fringes, where the lantern light met the encroaching darkness. His appearance was unassuming, yet there was an aura about him that commanded attention. As he introduced himself to me, his eyes held a depth, a wisdom that seemed to span decades, suggesting that our home's secrets were as familiar to him as old friends.

"Quincy!" I heard my husband exclaim. "I need your help! Pettie, our daughter, is missing!"

Grant's face, which had been a mask of grim determination, softened momentarily upon seeing Quincy. Their exchange was brief, words spoken in hushed tones, but the weight of their conversation was palpable.

With a simple nod, Quincy affirmed his participation, adding his strength and resolve to our desperate mission. His presence, somehow both reassuring and enigmatic, made me wonder about the depths of knowledge he held about Laurel House and its grounds. Yet, even with everyone's combined efforts, the gnawing question remained: would we ever see our dear Pettie again?

That agonizing uncertainty overwhelmed me. The weight of it, the sheer terror and helplessness, became too much to bear.

My voice, raw and filled with despair, erupted in a scream that echoed through the vastness of our estate, reverberating the pain of a mother's broken heart.

Again and again, I screamed, each cry a manifestation of my deepest fears.

The night's turmoil reached its peak with the hurried footsteps of the local doctor, who had been summoned to address my deteriorating state. His face, lined with years of experience, showed a mix of professional concern and genuine sympathy. With gentle assurance, he administered a tonic, its purpose to soothe my shattered nerves.

The liquid's warmth spread through me, and the edges of reality began to soften, drawing me into a hazy lull. Yet, even as darkness encroached on my consciousness, faint, taunting whispers seemed to drift from the shadows, hinting at secrets and mysteries yet to be unraveled.

The confines of the room seemed to dissolve, the worried faces of those around me blurring into indistinct shapes, their voices mere echoes in a cavernous void. The weight of the day's events pressed down on me, each breath more laborious than the last, as the encroaching shadows of despair threatened to consume my very being.

As I hovered on the precipice of consciousness, the dissonant hum of reality began to recede, replaced by an all-encompassing silence. This stillness, which might have been a respite, was shattered by chilling whispers that slithered into my ears, winding their way through my mind like malevolent serpents.

We have Pettie... the voices hissed, each word dripping with malevolence. *She won't be coming back. We need her...we need you too...*

The finality of their claim gripped my heart with icy fingers, sending waves of dread crashing over me. *Were these the spirits of Laurel House? Had they truly ensnared my precious child?*

Despair threatened to drown me, the whispers serving as a haunting lullaby, drawing me deeper into the abyss. Their sinister message became an anchor, pulling me further from the waking world and into the realm of nightmares.

The ghosts of our horrible home had staked their claim, and the horrifying reality settled in.

Pettie had been right all along. The whispers were real, and they were no good.

No good for anyone...

Chapter Six—Grant

The first rays of dawn broke over Bryan Bay, casting a soft, golden hue upon the town. But the beauty of the new day did little to lift the heavy pall that had settled over us. News of Pettie's disappearance had spread like wildfire, and by morning, the entire town had rallied to our aid.

Main Street, usually bustling with the morning's commerce, was transformed. Shopkeepers shuttered their stores, and residents poured out of their homes, maps in hand, ready to join the search. The atmosphere was thick with a mix of determination and dread. Every corner echoed with whispered prayers and hushed discussions, all united in a singular purpose—finding Pettie.

The nearby woods, with their towering trees and dense underbrush, became the primary focus of the search. Groups of volunteers, marked with bright armbands for visibility, ventured into the forest.

Their voices, calling out for Pettie, were a constant refrain, mixing with the songs of the morning birds.

Fields took on a more ominous tone. Rows of townsfolk, hands linked, combed through the tall grasses methodically, ensuring no stone was left unturned.

But with the town's unity came unwanted attention. Reporters, sensing a story that gripped the heart, descended upon Bryan Bay. Their cameras captured the raw emotion of the search, but their presence was a stark reminder of the gravity of our situation.

Back at Laurel House, my beloved Virginia was cocooned in our bedroom. The strain of the previous night had taken its toll. The once vibrant woman I knew was now subdued, her eyes red-rimmed from tears, her face etched with worry. The doctor had given her a sedative to help her rest, but even in her sleep, I could see the lines of tension on her face.

Each hour that passed without finding Pettie weighed heavily on my heart. But amidst the despair, the town's unwavering support was a beacon of hope. We were not alone in our search; we were one community, bound together by a shared purpose and a desperate hope.

Time, a healer for most wounds, became my tormentor. Each sunrise and sunset marked not just the passage of days, but a growing chasm of despair.

Days blurred into weeks, and the large crowds that once filled our grounds and the woods beyond dwindled. The fervor of the initial search faded, replaced by the mundane routines of daily life. Bryan Bay had mourned with us, but life, as it often does, moved on.

But not for me. Not for Alan. And certainly not for Virginia.

Alan, my stoic boy, became my shadow. Every morning, equipped with a small satchel of supplies, we'd set out, our mission unwavering. The woods, once a haven of beauty, now loomed large with secrets and shadows. We called out, our voices growing hoarse, praying for any sign, any hint of Pettie.

Then there was Quincy. The old gardener, with his wisdom and age-worn face, would sometimes join our search. His appearances were sporadic, often emerging from the garden's depths with an uncanny sense of timing. There was a gravity to him, a weight of knowledge that both comforted and unnerved me. He never spoke much during these searches, but his presence was a silent testament to his bond with our family.

But the most heartbreaking transformation was Virginia's.

Gone was the spirited woman I had married. In her place was a specter, a shadow of her former self. She had taken to a chair by the window, the very window that overlooked the garden where Pettie had last been seen.

Day in and day out, she sat there, her gaze unwavering, her hope undying. Her meals went untouched, her once vibrant voice reduced to murmurs and whispers. I'd catch her sometimes, speaking softly, as if in conversation with the very spirits that might hold the answers.

Her sanity, frayed by grief and despair, hung by a thread. At night, I'd hear her sobbing, interspersed with laughter - a chilling, hollow laughter that echoed the depths of her pain. It tore at my soul to see her this way, to feel so powerless against the tide of anguish that had engulfed us.

The walls of Laurel House seemed to close in, the weight of its history, its secrets, pressing down on us. Whispers from the past taunted us, reminding us of the price we were paying. And through it all, one haunting question remained: Where was Pettie?

One evening, as the sun cast long, somber shadows across the hallways of Laurel House, I encountered Leo. The cat had been a playful, almost mischievous presence since our arrival. But today, something was different. His strange eyes, one blue, one green, usually sparkling, held an odd, manifest darkness, a depth I hadn't noticed before. As I approached him, trying to soothe him with gentle strokes, he suddenly lunged at me, his claws outstretched, aiming for my face. Granted I'd had only a few run ins with the cat previous to this but none of those run ins were vicious. I never felt threatened by the animal—until now.

I recoiled, barely escaping the full force of his fury, feeling the sharp sting as one of his claws grazed my cheek. Shocked, I stumbled backward, watching as Leo hissed, his fur standing on end, every inch of him radiating malevolence.

"Mr. Boyd!" I yelled, my voice echoing through the house, "Take this cat away! I won't have such a beast in the house!" But as the words left my mouth, a heart-wrenching cry pierced the air.

Alan, my brave young son, rushed to Leo's side, scooping him up and cradling him protectively. Tears streamed down his face, mingling with the anger in his eyes.

"No, Father! You can't send Leo away! He's Pettie's cat! She loved him! What will she say when she comes back?"

Every word he uttered was like a dagger to my heart. The weight of our shared grief, the pain of Pettie's absence, it all came rushing back.

"Alan," I began, my voice trembling, "I... I didn't mean to..."

But before I could finish, he turned on his heel and fled, Leo clutched tightly to his chest. I heard the soft thud of his footsteps as he ascended the staircase, followed by the resounding slam of his bedroom door.

I stood there, in the dimly lit hallway, the weight of my actions pressing down on me. It wasn't just Leo I had pushed away. It was Alan. My own son. The walls of Laurel House, already thick with secrets and memories, now bore witness to another moment of heartbreak.

The atmosphere in Laurel House had grown stifling, each room seemingly holding its breath. With a heavy heart, I approached Virginia's chamber, gently knocking before entering. The room was dim, the curtains drawn, casting a muted glow from the outside world. Virginia sat in her usual spot, her gaze fixed on the gardens, her silhouette framed by the window.

In my hand, I clutched my mother's pendant, an heirloom passed down through generations. Its intricate design and the memories it held always brought me comfort during my darkest hours.

"Virginia," I began softly, hoping to break her trance. "I have something for you. It was my mother's."

She turned her head ever so slightly, her eyes, once full of life, now dull and distant. As I placed the pendant in her hand, I saw a brief flicker of a sad smile tugging at the corners of her lips. Yet, she remained silent, the weight of our daughter's absence rendering her voiceless.

"Maybe it will protect you. I love you, Virginia. Don't give up hope, darling. We'll find her. I will bring Pettie home, I promise."

She clutched me desperately and cried with her all heart. I held her and cried along with her. When she fell asleep, I settled her back down into her bed and feeling a renewed sense of urgency, I decided to seek out Quincy.

If there was anyone who knew about the mysteries of this land, the whispered tales of the Midnight Veil group, it was him. Perhaps they held the key to Pettie's disappearance.

As I traversed the expansive grounds, my determination grew. The wind whispered through the trees, carrying with it secrets I was yet to uncover. Finally, in the distance, I spotted Quincy, his figure outlined by the setting sun.

"Quincy!" I called out, my voice filled with a mix of hope and desperation. "I need answers, and I believe you have them. Tell me about the Midnight Veil. Are they responsible for taking Pettie?"

Quincy turned to face me; his expression inscrutable. The weight of the stories he held, the truths he had witnessed, all lay heavily upon him. And in that moment, I knew my search for answers was about to take a dark and twisted turn.

The air grew colder as Quincy led me further into the heart of the garden, away from the manicured lawns and flower beds I had come to know. The atmosphere was thick with anticipation, and each step felt like a descent into a forgotten world.

"We shouldn't be here," Quincy murmured, his voice barely above a whisper. But there was a determination in his eyes that told me he had made up his mind. "This is no place for the living."

Pushing aside thick overgrowth and tangled vines, we came upon a clearing, dominated by an ancient stone circle. The stones, worn by time and weather, stood tall and imposing, their surfaces covered in moss and cryptic markings. The very earth seemed to hum beneath my feet, and I felt an overwhelming sense of reverence.

"This... this is the heart of Laurel House's secrets," Quincy said, his voice trembling. "Few alive know of this place, and fewer still have dared to step foot here."

I looked around, trying to process the gravity of what lay before me. The circle, though silent, felt alive, pulsating with energy that seemed both ancient and foreboding. "What is this place, Quincy?" I asked, my voice echoing in the stillness.

He sighed deeply, choosing his words carefully. "This, Grant, is where the Midnight Veil once performed their rituals, attempting to bridge the divide between our world and the next. Their practices, stealing the souls of the innocence, though reprehensible, made them strong and unstoppable for a time."

The air grew tense as Quincy began to speak, his voice low and filled with a mixture of reverence and fear. "The Midnight Veil was no mere gathering of curious townsfolk, Grant. They were seekers of forbidden knowledge, dabblers in the arcane, and their thirst for power knew no bounds. They fought hard to keep this land but your great grandfather bought it lock, stock and barrel. For all their power, they neglected to pay their taxes and the land was sold by the bank. That's how the Sullivans got involved. That's how I remember it."

I listened intently, every word echoing in the stillness of the stone circle. "They believed that the innocent dead, victims of yellow fever and polio epidemics, held untapped power, and that by collecting the souls of the children, by controlling them, they could achieve dominion over forces beyond mortal comprehension."

Quincy paused, taking a deep breath, as if steeling himself for what was to come. "One of their most sinister rituals was known as 'grave soaking'. They would lay upon the graves of children and the innocent, believing that by doing so, they could absorb the souls' purity and innocence."

A shiver ran down my spine, the weight of his words pressing down on me. The very thought of such a ritual, performed here, on this very ground, was too much to bear.

"Why children, Quincy? Why the innocent?" I asked, my voice barely above a whisper.

Quincy's eyes darkened. "Because, Grant, in their twisted beliefs, the souls of the innocent held the most power. By harnessing such souls, the Midnight Veil believed they could command greater evils, entities beyond our understanding."

"I'm not a religious person but even I believe that when we die, we go to heaven, or hell. Or we go to sleep. How is it possible that these souls could be disturbed in such a way?"

"Humans are complicated creatures, Grant. We made of three parts, body, spirit and soul. The body dies and is buried or collected in some way. At that time, the spirit, if it belongs to God, rises to be with him. It escapes the grave. However, there is a small pieces of a person left behind, it is called the soul. The soul contains your personality, dreams that didn't come true, destiny foisted. The magic of you remains. To a witch or a warlock, these kind of souls have their uses. And those uses include commanding dark and dangerous things.

I felt a wave of nausea, the implications of his words crashing down on me. The very ground we stood on, the home I had brought my family to, was tainted by these unspeakable acts. "And Pettie?" I choked out, my mind racing. "Is this why she's gone? Have they stolen her soul?"

Quincy looked away, his face a mask of sorrow. "The spirits remember, Grant. The echoes of the past still resonate here, and Pettie drew their attention. She is innocent and open and that makes her the perfect target."

The dense atmosphere of the garden seemed to close in around me as I tried to process Quincy's words. "But why Pettie? She's just a little girl," I stammered, my voice tinged with desperation. "They were grave soakers, right? They took power from the dead, not the living! Pettie isn't dead. She's alive!"

Quincy's face was etched with pain, his eyes glistening with unshed tears. "That's right, Grant. Keep the faith, son. But dead or not, they do not care. The Midnight Veil never went away, not really, but in their quietness, they grew stronger. And now, they might be powerful enough to not just tap into the energy of the dead, but to pull a living soul through the veil. Imagine the power that would give them. A living soul in their command?"

My heart felt like it was being crushed, the weight of realization pressing down on me. The implications of what he was saying, the thought of my innocent Pettie in the hands of such malevolent forces, was unbearable.

My knees buckled, and I found myself sinking to the ground amidst the overgrown grass and wildflowers of the ancient stone circle.

Tears streamed down my face, each one a testament to the overwhelming grief and helplessness I felt. My sobs echoed through the garden, a haunting lament for a father's lost child.

Quincy, the old gardener with secrets of his own, moved closer. He placed a comforting hand on my shoulder, his touch firm yet gentle. "I'm so sorry, Grant," he whispered, his voice thick with emotion. "But you must think of Alan. Think of your other child. They won't stop with Pettie."

And at hearing those words, I was face down in the dirt, weeping for all my worth.

Chapter Seven—Virginia

The dim, muted light of dawn filtered through the heavy drapes, casting a soft, ghostly glow throughout the hall. My footsteps were quiet, almost hesitant, as I descended the grand staircase, drawn by an inexplicable urge to sit by the window.

The house was silent, save for the faint murmur of voices and clinking of pots from the kitchen. The comforting aroma of freshly baked bread wafted through the air, a stark contrast to the palpable melancholy that had settled over Laurel House.

As I approached the window, a chill ran down my spine. There, framed by the open front door, stood Pettie. At least I think it was Pettie. The way the sun shone behind her, face was covered in shadow. I stood stock still. Was I hallucinating again? The daily sedative had taken its toll on my mind, on my sanity.

"Pettie? Is that you, baby?"

Her once vibrant blue dress clung to her small frame, drenched and dripping as though she had been caught in a torrential downpour. But there was no rain outside, no sign of any water. Her golden locks, usually neatly tied up with an oversized ribbon, hung wet and limp around her face. Her shoes, caked in mud, left small puddles on the polished wooden floor.

For a moment, time seemed to stand still. My heart raced, and a mixture of relief, joy, and dread surged through me.

"Pettie?" I whispered, my voice trembling with a mix of hope and fear. My mouth felt dry and stale.

She didn't respond, her pale blue eyes staring blankly ahead, her expression distant and vacant. The realization that this might not be a joyous reunion began to dawn on me.

What had happened to my precious daughter during her disappearance? And what unspeakable horrors had she witnessed?

Tears blurred my vision, a hot cascade spilling over my cheeks as an overwhelming urge to embrace my lost child consumed me. Every fiber of my being yearned to cradle her, to bask in the familiarity of her warmth, to anchor myself to the undeniable truth of her presence.

Yet, as I moved closer, a heart-wrenching coldness began to envelop me. Her eerie stillness, drenched appearance, the empty gaze — it all painted a macabre tableau that made my soul quiver. The harrowing truths lurking in the shadows of this reunion threatened to drown me in a sea of despair and disbelief.

The room seemed to stand still, its very walls holding their breath as I gazed at the vision before me.

"Pettie?" My voice, trembling with a mixture of hope and disbelief, broke the silence. "It's Mother, darling. Can you see me?" My heart raced, every beat echoing the intensity of the moment. "Is it truly you, my love?" The desperation in my voice was palpable, every word a plea for reality to align with the sight before me.

Without thinking, I shouted, "Grant! Hurry, come down!" The urgency in my voice roused the household. Within moments, the once quiet foyer was a cacophony of voices - the family, the staff, all gathered, their faces a mosaic of shock, joy, and incredulity.

Tears of relief flowed freely as we encircled Pettie, the room echoing with cries of happiness and astonishment.

Gently, I took her by the hand, guiding her upstairs. The dampness of her clothes, the distant look in her eyes, all demanded immediate care. "Let's get you cleaned up, darling," I whispered, drawing a bath for her, the warm water hopefully serving to wash away the mysterious events of her absence.

Downstairs, I could hear Grant's voice, filled with a mix of relief and concern, as he called for the doctor.

The news of Pettie's miraculous return spread like wildfire, and soon the house was surrounded.

The townspeople, our neighbors, friends, even strangers, all congregated, their faces pressed against windows, their voices a blend of wonder and curiosity. Everyone wanted to see the little Sullivan girl who had vanished and now, against all odds, had returned.

The dim light from the bedside lamp cast a soft glow over Pettie's face. Her once radiant eyes, always alight with mischief and curiosity, now looked dull and distant. I tried, time and again, to penetrate that barrier, to reach the daughter I once knew.

"Sweetheart, where have you been? Can you tell me what happened?" My voice trembled with a mix of hope and desperation. But she remained silent, her gaze fixed on something far away, unreachable.

The doctor, a kind, elderly man with decades of experience, carefully examined her. He listened to her heart, checked her reflexes, and looked deep into her eyes, searching for a clue. "Physically, she seems fine, Mrs. Sullivan," he said, his voice filled with a mix of relief and perplexity. "But her pulse... it's fainter than it should be. And her skin," he added, touching her arm gently, "is much too cold. She must stay warm, be sure she drinks her broth regularly. It will help strengthen her. Maybe then she'll be able to tell us what happened to her. Poor thing."

Grant, our unwavering rock, approached Pettie with a tenderness that belied his growing despair. He gently took her cold hand into his, murmuring soft assurances, each word dripping with raw emotion.

But as he searched her eyes for a glimmer of recognition, it became hauntingly clear: she was gazing beyond him, past the confines of our reality, into a shadowed realm that we could neither comprehend, nor access. The distance between father and daughter, once bridged by love and shared memories, now felt like an immeasurable void, chilling and profound.

Seeing my husband struggling to reach Pettie shattered my already broken heart.

Grant knelt before Pettie, his face a mere breath away from hers, trying to capture her gaze. "Pettie," he whispered, his voice trembling with a mix of hope and desperation. "It's me, Father. Do you remember the song I used to sing to you at bedtime? The one about the moon and stars?"

She continued to stare, her once radiant blue eyes now dulled and seemingly void of life, looking past him as if he were a mere shadow.

"Pettie," Grant's voice cracked, tears forming in his eyes, "please, sweetheart, say something. Anything. Just let me know you're still in there."

But she remained silent, her gaze unwavering, leaving Grant to grapple with the chilling realization that while his daughter might physically be back, her spirit seemed trapped elsewhere.

Alan, with the innocent perceptiveness only children possess, could sense the shift in the atmosphere. The joy of his sister's return was overshadowed by the eerie transformation she had undergone. He'd peek into her room, his face a blend of longing and fear, and then retreat, keeping a cautious distance.

The house, once filled with the joyful noise of a reunited family, now echoed with a haunting silence, punctuated only by the unanswerable questions that hung heavy in the air.

The veil of night brought with it an unsettling transformation to Laurel House.

As the last rays of sunlight disappeared, the soft, murmuring whispers that once danced at the periphery of our home now invaded its very core. The once comforting walls seemed to breathe with an eerie life of their own, every creak and groan echoing with the voices of the unseen.

The gas lamps flickered as if reacting to an unseen breeze, their flames casting quivering shadows that danced and played on the walls, hinting at forms just beyond perception.

The air grew cold, each breath I took forming a visible mist despite the warmth of the season. The once familiar rooms of the house seemed to twist and change in the dim light, corners appearing darker, hallways stretching longer.

Everywhere I went, the whispers followed, an incessant chorus of voices, some beseeching, some taunting. They grew louder, more insistent, as if trying to convey a message just beyond my comprehension.

The very atmosphere of the house felt charged, thick with anticipation, as if waiting for something – or someone – to emerge from the shadows.

I clutched my shawl tighter around me, every instinct urging me to seek the safety of light and company. Yet, I couldn't shake off the feeling that we were no longer alone in our home, that the boundaries between the living and the dead had blurred, and the spirits of my husband's forgotten past had come calling.

Creeping towards Pettie's room, every fiber of my being screamed at me to turn back, but a force beyond my understanding pulled me forward. As the door creaked open, a chilling, almost tangible mist filled the room, and the muted glow of the moon painted everything in a spectral hue.

Before me, a grotesque phantom materialized at the foot of my daughter's bed.

Its face, obscured by a hood of tattered ceremonial garb, dripped with an ancient darkness, its very presence seeming to drain the warmth from the room. It hovered in place, ethereal fingers extending, inching closer to Pettie's innocent form.

My heart threatened to leap from my chest as I watched, paralyzed, the line between the living and the dead now terrifyingly blurred.

Every tick of the clock felt like an eternity as our gazes locked. Those soulless, glowing eyes bored into mine, conveying a message that sent shards of ice through my veins.

A voice, eerily distant and chillingly clear, murmured, "You for her. You for her..."

The words echoed, their malevolent promise wrapping around me like a cold shroud. And then, with a rush of shadowy tendrils, the figure vanished, leaving behind an oppressive void.

"Leave her alone! Get away from Pettie!" I screamed and to my horror, it whispered hateful words to me but at least it seemingly disappeared.

My heart raced wildly, every beat echoing the dread that now consumed me, anchoring me to a moment of unparalleled fear.

And all the world went black as small hands encircled me.

Chapter Eight—Alan

The quiet of night was always deceptive in Laurel House. I remember waking up to the muted sound of footsteps, a soft, rhythmic tapping echoing through the corridor.

I poked my head out of my bedroom door and spotted Mother, her silhouette illuminated by the pale moonlight filtering through the tall windows. She seemed lost, her gaze distant, feet shuffling, leading her nowhere in particular. And she was going to collapse at any moment. Her slender figure swayed for a moment before she did indeed pass out.

Once I caught her, I didn't know what to do. *Cry out and wake up Pettie? Would she even hear us?* I wasn't sure my sister was even alive anymore. I never saw her eat or drink. She didn't go to the bathroom, or even close her eyes. Sometimes she barely blinked.

And now here Mother was poised outside her open door collapsing in my arms. Just like that, Father appeared. How had he known we needed his help?

"Alan, I have her. Mother will be okay. Get the door for me and then go back to bed," he whispered, but his voice was laced with concern, not reprimand. Together, we gently took hold of Mother, her frailty evident, guiding her back to her room.

I did as I was told, but it took what seemed like an eternity to go back to sleep. Why had I woken up to begin with?

Morning light unveiled the aftermath of the previous night's eeriness. Pushing the heavy bedroom door open, I found Mother sitting by her vanity, her fingers caressing the delicate lace of an old photograph. I approached tentatively.

"Mother? It's me, Alan."

She looked up, her eyes, once vibrant and full of life, now mirrored the same haunted look I'd seen in Pettie's. "Alan," she whispered, her voice fragile, as if on the verge of shattering. "Let's not talk about anything troubling. You should go have breakfast with your sister. She needs her family. Mother isn't feeling well this morning."

My heart ached, seeing her like this. "But Mother, we must talk. We can't just—"

Before I could finish speaking, a sharp cracking sound sliced through our conversation.

We both turned to find the large ornate mirror on the far wall slowly spider-webbing with cracks. It started from the center, radiating outward, the once clear reflection now distorted and fragmented. I could see myself splintering before my own eyes. I jumped back, startled.

The room, filled with the foreboding atmosphere of the house, seemed to close in on us. Mother's eyes darted around, fear evident.

"They will come for her," she whispered, her voice trembling. "They will come for me too. They must be in the house already."

Unsure what to make of this I left her and she did not stop me. In fact, I was pretty sure she'd forgotten I had been talking to her. I considered telling Father about the mirror and Mother's strange behavior but thought better of it. Father had enough on his mind already.

One evening, as the shadows lengthened and the sun's last rays were smothered by the encroaching darkness, a soft melody reached my ears. It was a lullaby, one that I recognized from our childhood. A simple rhyme about a moon and a star that danced with one another.

The one Pettie used to sing.

Was this real? Pettie hadn't spoken a word since she'd returned home. And where had she been? Was she ready to talk now?

I hesitated for a moment, the hairs on the back of my neck standing on end. There was something off about the tune. It was Pettie's voice, but the sweetness was replaced by a chilling, mournful undertone. Drawn to it, almost like a moth to a flame, I followed the sound.

The lullaby led me to a guest room—we seldom used it. We never had any guests anymore. The door was slightly ajar. The room was bathed in a gloomy twilight, the only light coming from the setting sun filtering through the lace curtains.

In the corner, on an old rocking chair, sat Pettie. She cradled the porcelain doll, its dress fabric faded and frayed from years of love and wear. The doll's glassy eyes seemed to reflect the dim light, giving it an almost lifelike quality. She'd found the doll the first day we'd arrived here. I never liked it.

The temperature in the room was noticeably colder, a chill that seeped into my bones. I could see my breath, forming small puffs of mist in the air.

Pettie continued her song, seemingly unaware of my presence, her voice echoing in the cold, silent room.

"Pettie?" I ventured, my voice barely above a whisper, fearing to break the trance she was in. "What are you doing in here?"

But she continued, her voice weaving a tapestry of melancholy and memories, taking me back to a time when things were simpler, before the shadows of Laurel House took hold.

As I backed away from the room, trying to process the eerie scene I had just witnessed, the quiet hum of the house was replaced by faint, unintelligible whispers. All around me, whispers! Voices, dozens of voices. They were in my ears, in my mind, snapping at my neck. Invisible teeth! I could hear them clicking and snapping at me!

They seemed to emanate from the very walls. And on those walls, shadows danced and elongated in ways that defied the natural play of light and dark. Heart pounding, I tried to locate the source of the voices.

The whispers grew louder, more insistent. Each step I took intensified them, as if I was drawing closer to some unseen gathering. I reached the grand staircase, and it was there that the whispers became clearer, more distinct. They seemed to be beckoning me, urging me to follow.

Yes, this way. Come with us!

Without thinking, I began to descend, each step weighed down by a growing sense of dread.

Halfway down, I paused. The whispers now seemed to be coming from the open front door. Steeling myself, I approached the door, which stood slightly ajar. Pushing it open, I was met with a sight that chilled my blood.

The garden beyond was bathed in an otherworldly glow, and at the center stood Pettie, her back to me.

"Pettie? Weren't you just upstairs?" I whispered to her, afraid to speak too loudly, in case this wasn't Pettie at all.

Around her, the shadows seemed to move and shift, forming ghostly figures that whispered and murmured among themselves. They were reenacting some ancient, forgotten ritual, and Pettie was at its heart.

I wanted to call out to her, to pull her from whatever dark spell she was under, but my voice caught in my throat. I was paralyzed, unable to move, a mere spectator to the terrifying spectacle unfolding before me.

And then, just as suddenly as it had begun, it stopped. The figures dissipated, the gardens plunged back into darkness, and Pettie vanished before my eyes. I rushed to the edge of the garden, tempted to pursue her, find her.

But that's not Pettie! That's not my sister!

I ran back inside the house and quietly shut the front door. I turned the key and raced back up the stairs. My heart pounded in my chest, and I could hear my blood pulsing through my veins.

Tossing and turning beneath my sheets, sleep remained elusive. The stillness of the night was disrupted by an unsettling hum, gradually growing into a chorus of whispers that seemed to emanate from every corner of my room.

The very walls, the creaking floorboards beneath my bed, the rustling curtains; all conspired to carry those ghostly voices to my ears.

You for her. You for her.

The whispers murmured in chilling harmony, their voices intertwining, becoming almost melodic.

The Veil awaits, the sacrifice must be made. Decide!

My heart raced, every fiber of my being urging me to escape this auditory assault. But I was pinned down, not by any physical force, but by an overpowering curiosity. I strained to decipher the riddles, to understand the messages hidden within the cacophony.

Then, as abruptly as they began, the whispers ceased.

The room returned to its nocturnal quietude, but the weight of the revelations remained, pressing down on me like a suffocating blanket.

I lay there, wide-eyed, the chilling implications of the whispers echoing in my mind.

What sacrifice were they referring to? Was Pettie's sudden return and changed demeanor a part of some larger, more diabolical plan?

In the shrouded realm of sleep, I found myself standing at the edge of the overgrown garden. The moon hung low, casting a pallid light that made the shadows dance and twist in grotesque patterns. The very air was thick with tension, electric with anticipation.

There, amidst the ancient stone circle, stood a group of figures, their faces obscured by the flickering torchlight. Among them, shockingly, was a younger version of Mother, her eyes wide and filled with a mix of awe and fear. Her voice joined the others in a haunting chant that seemed to rise and swell with the wind.

In the center of the gathering, dominating the scene, was a stone altar, stained dark with age and perhaps more. The rhythmic beat of a drum combined with the chants, creating a hypnotic melody that held me in its grip. Around them, ceremonial fires blazed, their flames reaching skyward as if trying to touch the stars.

As the ritual reached its crescendo, a cloaked figure approached the altar, holding something delicate and shimmering in their hands. The collective chant grew louder, more urgent. And then, piercing the night, came a scream — raw, full of agony and despair.

It was a sound that no human should ever have to make or hear. Jolted awake, I found myself in my bed, drenched in sweat.

The echoes of that scream still lingered in my ears, its harrowing resonance making my heart race. The line between dream and memory blurred, leaving me with a sinking feeling that what I'd witnessed wasn't just a product of my imagination, but a glimpse into a dark chapter of Laurel House's past.

The morning sun did little to dispel the shadows that clung to the corners of my mind. The haunting images of the ritual, the chilling scream, all replayed in an endless loop.

I needed answers, and in my gut, I knew Pettie held some clue.

Finding her wasn't hard. She was in her dimly lit bedroom, her blue eyes staring blankly ahead. Taking a deep breath, I approached her.

"Pettie," I began, my voice shaking despite my best efforts to keep it steady, "Do you know about the ritual in the garden? About the altar?"

For a moment, there was no response. Then, slowly, she turned her gaze to me. There was a flash of recognition, a spark of the sister I once knew. Her hand shot out, gripping mine with a surprising strength. Her fingers were cold, but her eyes held an urgency that belied her frailty.

She said nothing but stared at me with eyes that seemed to read my very soul. And just as quickly, she loosened her grip and walked to the window. She ignored me, and terrified, I left her alone.

Alone. We were all alone in this house. Each one of us, alone.

Chapter Nine–Virginia

The soft morning light filtered through the lace curtains, casting a delicate pattern on the wooden floor. The room was silent except for the occasional chirping of birds and the distant sounds of the household waking up. Nestled among the pile of letters on the ornate table by the window was a familiar envelope, sealed with Evelyn's personal wax stamp.

With trembling hands, I carefully opened it, the edges of the paper crisp beneath my fingertips. Evelyn's elegant script flowed across the page, every curve and line a testament to the urgency of her message.

"Dearest Virginia," the letter began, "I hope this letter finds you in better spirits than the rumors that have reached me. The news of Pettie's mysterious disappearance and return has deeply unsettled me, and I am compelled to write to you."

"It's the Midnight Veil that truly concerns me. I've spent weeks pouring over old town records and speaking with some of the elders there. The tales are disturbing. They speak of a group that believed in grave soaking, absorbing the energies of the departed, especially innocent souls like children. It's said they performed dark rituals, ones that took lives in the name of sacrifice. And the culmination of their descent into darkness was a mass suicide, right there, on your very property. But their leader, a figure spoken of in hushed tones and fearful glances, vanished, leaving a trail of dread in his wake."

"I urge you, Virginia, be cautious. Do not dismiss these tales as mere superstitions. There is a palpable darkness associated with the Midnight Veil, and I fear for your family's safety. Please, consider leaving Laurel House, at least for a time."

"With all my love and concern,"

Evelyn

I felt the weight of Evelyn's words like a physical force, pressing down upon my chest, making it hard to breathe. Each line of her letter, every word she penned, painted a terrifying picture that I couldn't ignore. The history of our house, the land it stood upon, was soaked in tales of darkness and despair.

The past was alive, whispering its secrets, and it was here, in our very home.

Grant, always the pragmatic one, was reluctant to believe. When I tried to share the revelations with him, he dismissed them, his voice filled with skepticism. "Old wives' tales," he'd say. "Evelyn has always had an active imagination."

But my sister's words weren't mere fiction. The cold drafts, the haunting lullabies, Pettie's altered state — all of it was connected, intertwined with the shadowy legacy of the Midnight Veil.

In my desperation, I reached out to Reverend Thomas from the Bryan Bay church. His reputation for understanding matters both spiritual and otherworldly made him my last beacon of hope. I penned a hasty note detailing our plight, and Mrs. Higgins, sensing the urgency, ensured its swift delivery.

The reverend's response was prompt. That very afternoon, he arrived at Laurel House. Reverend Thomas, his features lined with age and wisdom, listened intently as I recounted the events of the past weeks, the eerie occurrences, and Evelyn's letter.

He took a moment, his fingers steepled in thought, before finally speaking, "Virginia, there are places in this world where the veil between the living and the dead is thin. This house, this land, seems to be one such place. We need to perform a cleansing, to push back against the shadows that threaten to consume."

With a solemn nod, he agreed to return at sundown, equipped with the tools of his faith: holy water, sacred scriptures, and an unwavering belief in the power of the divine.

His departure left me with a sliver of hope, a fragile belief that perhaps we could reclaim our home from the haunting grip of the past.

Yet, beneath that hope, a chilling dread lingered, whispering that the heart of the darkness has yet to reveal itself.

The evening sun, a fierce orange orb, dipped below the horizon, casting long, stretching shadows across Laurel House. The golden hue gave an eerie luminance to the mansion, making it seem like a beacon in a sea of encroaching darkness.

I hesitated at the entrance of the study, watching Grant. He sat deep in thought, his focus on the paperwork scattered across the mahogany table, the dim light from the desk lamp accentuating the lines of worry etched onto his face.

Taking a deep breath, I softly called out, "Grant."

He looked up, momentarily startled, as if pulled from another world. "Virginia? What is it?" he asked, his tone gentle yet distracted.

Mustering up the courage, I said, "Reverend Thomas will be coming tonight. He believes he can help us. He's convinced that a ritual can cleanse the house."

A look of disbelief, mingled with a hint of annoyance, flashed across his face. "Virginia," he began, choosing his words carefully, "do you truly think that some chants and rituals will rid us of this... nightmare? That it will help our family? All this mysticism..."

"Grant, it's not mysticism. It's faith! We need this! The children need this!"

My heart ached, but I took a step closer, the urgency of the situation propelling me forward. I took his roughened hands in mine, trying to convey all the hope and despair I felt. "Grant, I'm scared. Every day, every night, this house tightens its grip on us. On Pettie. On Alan." My voice broke, but I continued, "We have to try. We owe it to our family. We can't just stand by and let this darkness consume us."

Grant sighed, pulling me into an embrace. The warmth of his body was a stark contrast to the cold dread that had settled in my heart. "Alright," he whispered into my hair, his voice filled with resignation and love, "For our family. We'll try."

Grant and I stood in his study, the weight of our discussion pressing on us. But as we spoke, a sudden movement caught my eye. Pettie, who had been so still, so silent by the window, now stood. The gentle little girl we once knew seemed almost foreign as she stared intently out into the gathering darkness. Her once vibrant blue eyes, which used to dance with mischief and joy, now appeared clouded, lost. It was as if they peered into another world, one that we couldn't see or comprehend.

"Pet...Pettie?" Grant's voice, usually so firm, wavered with a mix of hope and fear.

She didn't respond, her attention ensnared by whatever vision held her gaze.

The room's temperature seemed to drop, and I could see our breaths in the cold air. Alan, ever the perceptive child, clutched his toy to his chest and began to edge backward, towards the door.

As Alan's footsteps grew fainter, the heavy oaken doors leading into the study creaked open. The silhouette of a man, tall and imposing, framed by the dim hallway light, stepped into the room.

It was Reverend Thomas, his usual calm demeanor now replaced by a palpable sense of urgency. I was relieved that he had arrived, although Pettie's body language suggested she was not happy about the minister's arrival.

"Good evening, Mr. and Mrs. Sullivan," he greeted, though his voice held a gravitas that belied the pleasantries. "I returned as soon as I could. I am sorry for the delay. Ah, there is our little Pettie. Hello, child."

Of course, she did not speak. She hadn't spoken a word since her return. She didn't move, but at least she wasn't staring out the window anymore.

Grant, ever the skeptic, eyed the reverend with a hint of doubt. "So, what do you propose we do? Recite a few verses and hope the ghosts decide to leave?"

The reverend, undeterred by Grant's skepticism, replied, "Ghosts? I don't believe in ghosts, Mr. Sullivan. There are other things though. The bible tells us that there are evil spirits, demons. But more than likely, there's nothing. Only the remnants of what was. The Midnight Veil had a grip on this property for many years. We must confront this residual energy head-on."

Residual energy? I had no idea what that meant, but I didn't like his tone. Was he trying to say that this was all in our imaginations?

I felt a shiver run down my spine. "Reverend, I'm scared. For my children, for Grant, for myself. Whatever is in this house, it's growing stronger."

The reverend nodded, his gaze firm. "Fear not, Mrs. Sullivan. We are here to fight this darkness. Together, with faith and determination, we will reclaim Laurel House from the clutches of the Midnight Veil."

Night enveloped Laurel House, and what was once a haven became a place of shadows and uncertainty. The rooms, with their familiar furnishings, took on a more sinister appearance under the flickering candlelight. And then, as if on cue, the whispers started.

Soft at first, like a gentle caress against the ear, they grew louder, more urgent, their eerie murmurs seeping from the walls, the floors, even the very air we breathed. The boundary between the past and present, the living and the dead, seemed to blur, and I clung to Grant, hoping against hope that we could confront the haunting specter of the Midnight Veil.

Reverend Thomas had set up a circle of candles in the main drawing room, and as he began to recite the sacred verses, the very walls seemed to pulse and breathe.

Was I hearing things?

The servants refused to be involved in this and had quietly gathered outside to wait for the service to be over. That's when the loud footsteps began running overhead.

Who is that? Alan was sitting on the sofa. Pettie stared at us from the corner by her favorite window. Everyone else was outside of the house.

Grant, usually the skeptic, turned pale, his ears finally tuning into the sinister symphony that had plagued our family. "Do you hear that?" he whispered, his voice quivering.

Alan, clutching his teddy bear, tried to block out the sound, pressing his small hands against his ears. But the voices were relentless, and tears streamed down his face as he cried out in fear. I raced to his side and put my arm around his shoulders. He pressed his face against my skirt, and I did my best to comfort him.

Even as chaos reigned, Pettie remained eerily still, her focus locked onto the minister. The dull blue of her eyes seemed to gleam with an inner fire, a stark contrast to her pale, emotionless face. It was as if she was channeling the very energy causing the upheaval around us. Could that be true?

Reverend Thomas, taking in the scene, began to chant in a language I couldn't recognize, his voice rising above the cacophony, commanding and powerful. The very walls of Laurel House seemed to groan in response, the timbers creaking and the floorboards shifting beneath our feet.

Grant, attempting to shield me from the flying debris, cried out, "What is happening, Reverend? What have they done to our daughter?"

But the reverend was lost in his incantations, his eyes closed, beads of sweat forming on his brow. As he chanted, the air grew denser, and a low, resonating hum filled the house, drowning out even the loudest crashes.

Suddenly, Pettie's voice, clear and chilling, cut through the noise. "Leave!" she hissed, her voice echoing and distorted, not quite her own. It was as if multiple voices spoke in unison, each layered over the other.

The very foundations of Laurel House shook, and for a moment, it felt as though the entire structure would come crashing down. The oppressive energy peaked, then, as suddenly as it had begun, it receded, leaving behind an unsettling silence. The reverend, drained but resolute, opened his eyes, looking directly at Pettie.

"This is just the beginning," he whispered.

Reverend Thomas, his face a mask of determination, continued his chant, but the house, or whatever entity that had taken residence within it, fought back with a vengeance.

The atmosphere was thick with tension and terror, the boundary between the living and the dead blurring as the battle for Laurel House raged on.

The once methodical chants of the reverend were suddenly silenced by a deafening crash. A heavy, ornate vase had taken flight from its perch, striking him squarely in the back. He crumpled to the floor, gasping for breath, his face contorted in pain.

For a moment, time seemed to stand still. The malevolent energy that had consumed Laurel House appeared to revel in its triumph, casting an almost tangible, smothering shadow over us all. The reverend, gathering the remnants of his strength, managed to rise to his knees, his eyes wide with terror.

"I cannot help you," he rasped, fear evident in his trembling voice. "The evil in this house... it's too strong. It's too strong! She cannot be saved!" And with those final words, he staggered to his feet and fled, leaving us to face the darkness alone.

"No! Reverend! You must help her!" I pleaded with him to no avail. He was gone, leaving his candles and his bible behind.

The weight of our circumstances bore down on me, and a crushing despair took hold.

My legs gave way, and I found myself sinking to the floor, tears streaming down my face. The realization that we were trapped, prisoners in our own home, was overwhelming.

I looked at my family, at Grant trying in vain to connect with Pettie, at Alan, whose young eyes held a depth of fear no child should ever experience and felt an aching helplessness.

Grant, his voice choked with emotion, softly called out to our daughter. "Pettie, please, speak to me." But she remained distant, her gaze fixed on something we couldn't see. With a mixture of desperation and tenderness, he gently lifted her into his arms, holding her close, his tears falling onto her pale face.

The sound of soft footsteps approached, and Mrs. Higgins, our loyal housekeeper, rushed to my side. Her warm embrace was a small comfort in the cold, oppressive atmosphere that had taken hold of Laurel House. "We'll find a way, ma'am," she whispered, her voice filled with determination. "We won't let them take her."

But as I looked around at the shattered remnants of our once-happy home, hope felt like a distant memory. The echoes of the past, the haunting whispers, and the relentless grip of the Midnight Veil seemed insurmountable.

And for the first time, I truly questioned if we would ever find a way out of this nightmarish reality.

The room seemed to close in around me, the weight of our situation pressing heavily on my chest. The silence was deafening, broken only by our ragged breaths and the distant howling of the wind outside.

I grabbed Grant's arm, my voice filled with desperation. "We have to leave, Grant. We must leave this cursed place. Laurel House is not our home anymore."

Grant looked deep into my eyes, the pain evident in his gaze. "You're right," he whispered, his voice hoarse. "We can't stay here. Not after everything that's happened."

But as we began to make plans, a small voice, filled with a haunting clarity, interrupted us. "They won't let her go, Mother," Alan said, his face pale, eyes wide with terror. "She belongs here. If we leave, they will take her again."

The room went cold. I turned to face my son, my heart pounding in my ears. "Alan, why would you say such a thing? How could you possibly know that?"

He looked down, his small frame shaking with fear. "The Whispers," he murmured, almost inaudibly. "They talk to me. All the time. They say 'you for her.' Over and over. 'You for her,' Mother. That's what they want."

Tears streamed down my face as the full weight of his words settled in my soul.

The malevolent forces that had taken hold of our home, of our family, were not going to let go easily.

We were trapped in a nightmare with no end in sight.

Chapter Ten–Grant

The night wrapped Laurel House in a suffocating cloak of darkness, its oppressive weight hanging heavily over the vast expanse of the garden. An unnatural stillness held the air captive, stifling the usual chorus of crickets and the gentle rustling of nocturnal creatures. The only sound was the crunch of gravel beneath my boots, each step echoing like a lonely heartbeat in the silence.

Moonlight seeped through the dense canopy above, painting the path with fleeting shadows that seemed to dance and flicker with a life of their own. The skeletal branches of the ancient trees reached out, their gnarled fingers casting dark, twisted patterns on the ground, as if trying to ensnare me in their grip.

With every step, an unsettling feeling of being observed grew stronger, as though invisible specters hovered just out of sight, their gaze fixed intently upon me. It felt as though the garden itself was holding its breath, waiting, watching.

Rounding a bend, a figure slowly materialized from the inky blackness. Quincy, his face etched with lines of age and wisdom, stood there as though he had materialized from the very fabric of the night. His eyes, usually so warm, now bore into mine with an intensity that was almost piercing.

"Grant," his voice rasped, low and filled with a gravity I hadn't heard before, "I've been waiting for you. The time has come to unveil what's been hidden for too long."

Quincy's gaze drifted, as if looking beyond the garden, beyond the present, to a time shrouded in shadows. The air grew even colder, if that was possible, and the oppressive silence deepened.

"In the early days of Bryan Bay," he began, the words rolling off his tongue slowly, as if each held a memory, a weight. His voice had the timbre of ancient wood, creaking and groaning under the force of a relentless wind, carrying tales from epochs long forgotten.

I felt that I should say something, but I wanted to hear more. Needed to hear the truth, at last.

"The town was abuzz with hushed conversations, with parents clutching their children close, eyes darting with suspicion. Whispers that started as mere ripples grew into waves of dread, speaking of children who vanished without a trace, of shadowy gatherings under the moon's cloak, and of a dark force so potent that it threatened to unravel the very essence of existence."

He paused, his gaze distant, as though he was transported to those bygone days. The very air around us seemed to thicken, charged with the energy of unspeakable truths.

"The Midnight Veil wasn't just a figment of an overactive imagination, nor tales spun by the elderly to keep mischievous children in line," Quincy's voice dropped to a haunting whisper, "They were very much real, more real than the ground we stand on. With an ambition that knew no bounds, they sought the purest of energies, the untouched souls of the innocent. Drawing them in, ensnaring them with promises or simply overpowering their will; they imprisoned these souls, casting them into a twilight realm – neither truly alive, nor completely departed."

The silence that followed was punctuated only by the distant hoot of an owl, a lone sentinel in this garden of secrets. I could feel the weight of generations of sorrow, of loss, pressing down on me.

Every rustling leaf, every whisper of the wind seemed to carry with it the cries of those lost souls.

"But why us? Why my family?" The question escaped my lips, desperation evident in my voice.

Quincy leaned in closer, his voice barely audible, as if even the walls had ears. "The house, this land, it's all connected. The spirits are drawn to it, to your family, because of the energy it holds. Your lineage is intertwined with the history of the Midnight Veil. Your ancestors, knowingly or unknowingly, played a part in this dark tapestry."

A chill ran down my spine. "That's not possible. You're saying my grandfather participated with these—these—witches!"

Quincy neither offered or an excuse or a denial.

"Then, what can I do? How can I end this?"

Quincy's gaze became distant, contemplative. "The answer, Grant, lies in understanding the past, confronting it, and finding a way to make peace with the restless souls here. Vanquishing the Midnight Veil will take a strong medium. We don't have anyone like that. Your mother tried to confront them but...now, the mantle falls on you."

My heart raced, each word from Quincy painting a horrifying picture of the past. "What about my mother?" I pressed, my voice barely above a whisper. "They killed her, didn't they? The Midnight Veil? The ghosts? Who?"

Quincy's eyes met mine, filled with a sorrow that seemed centuries old. "Your mother, Eleanor, had a gift, a sensitivity to the spirits. She could hear voices of the trapped souls, feel their pain. And she couldn't stand by and do nothing. She tried to break the cycle, to free those innocent souls from their eternal torment."

"Tell me! I think I deserve to know, Quincy!"

He paused, taking a shuddering breath. "She got too close, discovered too much. The Midnight Veil couldn't afford to have her reveal their secrets. And so, they silenced her. Before she passed on her knowledge, her determination, to you and your siblings, they kidnapped her. She's in their land, their realm, Grant."

The weight of his words felt overwhelming, but I knew, deep down, that escaping this legacy was not an option. The fate of my family, of Pettie and Alan, depended on it.

The cold night air became even more biting, each word from Quincy a dagger driving deeper into my heart. "This can't be real," I murmured, my voice trembling. "We're a normal family. We don't get tangled up in... in things like this."

Quincy's gaze was unwavering, his eyes reflecting the pale light of the moon. "There's no such thing as 'normal' when it comes to the veil between worlds, Grant. Your family, whether by fate or by choice, is bound to this place, to its history. To its spirits."

I took a step back, feeling the weight of the revelations pressing down on me. "Why didn't my father tell me? Why keep it a secret?"

Quincy sighed deeply, the sound echoing in the stillness of the garden. "Fear, perhaps. Or maybe hope. Hope that by ignoring it, by denying it, the past would stay buried. But the Whispers, they don't forget. They wait, they linger, always seeking a way in."

A shiver ran down my spine. I remembered the hushed tones, the late-night arguments between my parents, the distant look in my father's eyes. "He heard them, didn't he? The Whispers."

Quincy nodded slowly. "Yes, and he tried to shield you all from them. But they were persistent, especially when they sensed a connection, a vulnerability."

I sank to the ground, the weight of it all threatening to crush me. No doubt he was talking about some sort of vulnerability that I had. I didn't want to know if that were true.

"What do we do now?"

Quincy knelt beside me, placing a reassuring hand on my shoulder. "You face the Midnight Veil, Grant. You confront the past, the Whispers, and you find a way to break the cycle. For your family. For all those lost souls. It's the only way."

I didn't answer him but let the weight of his words just hang in the heavy air between us.

The path leading deeper into the garden was overgrown, a clear indication of years of neglect. Twisted branches seemed to reach out, as if warning us to stay away. Each step felt heavier, the weight of history, of the souls that had come before, pressing down on me.

We finally reached the sacrificial site, a clearing surrounded by ancient trees, their gnarled roots exposed, intertwining like a nest of vipers. In the center stood a stone altar, worn by time but still emanating a palpable energy.

Quincy stopped, his gaze fixed on the altar. The air around us grew still, the oppressive silence only broken by our ragged breaths. "This is where it all happened, Grant," he murmured, his voice carrying the weight of centuries.

I looked around, trying to imagine the rituals, the stolen souls, the cries that would have echoed through this very space. "Quincy," I began, "why bring me here?"

He turned to face me, and in that moment, I saw a profound sadness in his eyes, a pain that went beyond the confines of time. "I wanted you to see, to truly understand. I've been here, watching, waiting, for so long."

My heart raced. "Waiting for what?"

Quincy took a deep, ethereal breath. "For you to return. Someone with the authority to finally put an end to this curse. To free all those that trapped her. Free all of us."

I frowned, not fully grasping what he was saying. "Quincy, what do you mean? Free all of us? I don't understand."

He stepped closer, the moonlight casting an eerie glow on his face. "Grant," he whispered, his voice filled with sorrow, "I can't leave because I'm not truly here. Not in the way you are." The realization hit me like a tidal wave. The stories, the legends, they were all true. Quincy wasn't just an old man with tales of the past; he was a part of that past.

A spirit, trapped in this realm, bound to the very soil we stood on.

The weight of it all threatened to pull me under, but Quincy's spectral hand reached out, gripping my arm with a cold intensity.

"No! You can't be dead!" The thought of that sickened me, angered me, so much that clenched my fist, ready to punch something or someone.

Quincy grabbed my fists and shook his head. "You have the power to change things, Grant. To free us all. But you must be willing to face the darkness, to confront the Whispers and the malevolent forces that hold us here. Free us, Grant! Free us!"

Quincy began to fade before me. All that was left was a spectral silhouette, a strange collection of tiny lights that begin to lift away as his final words echoed in the stillness.

Free us... we remain...

I felt a chilling wind sweep through the clearing, the whispers growing louder, more insistent. Their haunting refrain a reminder of the battle that lay ahead. Each word from Quincy, each haunting truth about the Midnight Veil, my mother's tragic fate, and his own spectral existence felt like a dagger to my heart.

My mind raced, trying to process it all, but the magnitude of the horrors was overwhelming. A cold sweat broke out on my forehead, my pulse quickened, and a wave of dizziness threatened to topple me. The boundaries between the living and the dead, the past and the present, seemed to blur, and the very fabric of reality felt like it was tearing apart.

"No," I murmured, my voice hoarse with terror. "This can't be real. It's a nightmare."

But my own words were drowned out by the pounding of my heart and the rush of blood in my ears.

All that mattered was getting away, escaping the suffocating grip of the haunting truths that threatened to consume me. I had to take my family away and leave. We had to leave Laurel House—forever!

As I neared the edge of the garden, the oppressive atmosphere began to lift, replaced by the familiar sounds of the night.

Stumbling out from the dense canopy of the garden, Laurel House loomed before me, its grandeur now overshadowed by the dark secrets it harbored. The distant glow from its windows beckoned, promising safety and respite from the night's horrors. My heart raced, each pounding beat echoing the urgency of my need to reunite with my family.

My feet moved of their own accord, the gravel pathway beneath crunching in a frantic rhythm as I raced towards the entrance.

As I neared the house, the front door swung open, revealing Virginia, her face a canvas of relief and anxiety. Behind her, Alan clutched a small toy, his eyes wide and filled with fear. Mrs. Higgins, our loyal housekeeper, wrung her hands, her usual stoic demeanor replaced with genuine concern. But Pettie's absence was immediately felt, a void that sent a new wave of dread coursing through me.

"Grant!" Virginia's voice broke through the fog of my panic. "What happened? Where have you been? Why is Pettie not with you?"

The weight of the night's revelations bore down on me, each question amplifying the urgency to escape, to protect my family from the insidious grip of the Midnight Veil.

I took a moment, my breath coming in ragged gasps, trying to find the words to convey the gravity of what I'd learned. "Virginia," I began, my voice trembling, "Laurel House is not safe. We have to leave. Now."

She stared at me, her eyes searching mine for answers, trying to make sense of my urgency. "Grant, you're scaring me. What happened in the garden?"

I grabbed her shoulders, the cold reality of our situation seeping into every word. "The Midnight Veil, the Whispers, Quincy... it's all real. We're entwined in a dark legacy that reaches back through generations, and it wants our children."

Tears welled up in Virginia's eyes, her voice barely above a whisper. "They won't let us leave. I feel that in my bones."

I pulled her close, feeling her heartbeat against mine. "That's not true, Virginia. I should have never brought you here. I am sorry. It's not a home if it endangers our family. We must go, and we must go now."

In the distance, a chilling wail echoed through the halls, the very walls of Laurel House seeming to groan in anguish. The Whispers grew louder, their voices forming a cacophonous symphony of dread. It was clear: the battle for our souls, for our very lives, was reaching its climax.

The corridors of Laurel House, once filled with warmth and memories, now seemed like a labyrinth of shadows and dread. As Virginia and I hurriedly gathered essentials, I couldn't shake off the feeling that we were being watched, that every step was being monitored by unseen eyes.

Alan, clutching his teddy bear, looked up at me with wide, fearful eyes. "Daddy, the Whispers are getting louder," he murmured, his voice shaking.

I knelt down, cupping my son's face in my hands. "We're going to get out of here, okay? Stay close to me."

Virginia, clutching a bag filled with clothes and some food, joined us, her face pale but determined. "We need to find Pettie," she whispered, glancing down the hall towards her room. But as we approached Pettie's room, the door slowly swung open, revealing Pettie standing in the center, her gaze distant. She pulled away from us but made no sound.

A cold shiver ran down my spine. "Pettie," I began, my voice trembling, "we need to go. Now."

But as I reached out to her, the ground beneath us trembled, and a deafening roar filled the air, drowning out our cries. The walls seemed to close in on us, the very house resisting our escape. Thankfully she did not fight me.

Taking a deep breath, I mustered every ounce of courage and determination. With Virginia and Alan close behind, and carrying Pettie in my arms, we made our way to the main entrance. The once grand doors loomed ahead, our ticket to freedom. But as we approached, they slammed shut, the force of it sending a shockwave through the hall.

"No!" I shouted; desperation evident in my voice.

The house seemed to pulse with a dark energy, the air heavy with a sense of foreboding. The Whispers reached a crescendo, their voices intertwining in a chaotic symphony of despair.

Virginia held Alan close, her face a mask of terror. "We're trapped!" she exclaimed, her voice filled with panic.

I approached the doors, placing my hands on the cold, unyielding wood. I could feel the energy, the malevolent force trying to keep us inside. "We won't be imprisoned by this curse any longer!" I shouted, my voice echoing through the hall.

Drawing upon every ounce of strength, I pulled at the doors with all my might. For a moment, they resisted, but then, with a sudden jolt, they began to give way. A gust of cold wind rushed in, extinguishing the candles and plunging the hall into darkness.

From the shadows, Mrs. Higgins emerged, her usually kind face now stern and determined. "We cannot leave," she said, her voice oddly calm amidst the chaos. "Not yet. There is one more thing that needs to be done."

Virginia stepped forward, confusion evident in her eyes. "Mrs. Higgins, what are you talking about? Where did you get that necklace and pendant? Grant gave me that. It was his mothers."

With a heavy sigh, Mrs. Higgins began, "You shouldn't carry the burden here, Mrs. Sullivan. This house, its curse, it's been a burden for far too long. Your mother, Mr. Sullivan, Eleanor and I worked together, trying to free the souls trapped here. The devils here have taken many, including my Quincy. Now, it's time to end this."

Opening the locket, a soft, ethereal glow emanated from within. "The Midnight Veil is strong, their power can be broken, but it requires a sacrifice." Mrs. Higgins showed a winsome smile.

I stared at her, realization dawning. "No, Mrs. Higgins..."

Mrs. Higgins nodded. "To free the souls, to break the curse, one must be willing to give themselves to the Veil."

Virginia gasped, tears streaming down her face. "No, there has to be another way!"

Mrs. Higgins smiled sadly, "There isn't. His mother tried, and now, it's my turn. It should have been me before, but I was afraid. I failed Eleanor but I won't fail you!"

With a deep breath, she closed her eyes and began to whisper . The locket's glow intensified, casting an otherworldly light throughout the hall. The Whispers grew silent, the atmosphere electric with anticipation.

As the last word left Mrs. Higgins' lips, a blinding flash of light filled the room. When it subsided, she was gone, the locket lying on the floor, its glow extinguished.

The atmosphere within Laurel House grew dense with an all-consuming darkness. The walls, once sturdy and protective, now seemed to pulsate with a malevolent energy, each throb echoing the sinister chorus of the Whispers.

The very air around us grew thick, making every breath feel like a labor. Shadows twisted and writhed, manifesting into grotesque forms that seemed to reach out, attempting to ensnare us in their chilling grasp.

The once grand chandelier above us began to sway, its crystals clinking together to create an eerie melody that accompanied the Whispers. The portraits of past inhabitants seemed to come alive, their eyes following our every move with an accusing glare.

Virginia clutched Alan tighter, her eyes wide with terror. "The Whispers... they're everywhere!" she whispered hoarsely. "I hear them! Don't you hear them?"

Suddenly, the room grew colder, and a dense fog began to roll in, obscuring our vision. Out of the mist, shadowy figures began to emerge, their forms indistinct but their intent clear. They moved towards us, their movements slow but deliberate.

"We can't stay here!" I shouted, desperately searching for an escape route. But every door, every window seemed to be sealed shut, leaving us trapped with the malevolent entities.

Suddenly, Pettie, who had been silent all this time, began to sing. Her voice, soft and haunting, cut through the chaos, capturing the attention of everyone — even the Whispers.

It was an old lullaby, one that my mother used to sing, but it sounded different coming from my daughter — distorted and eerie.

Hush now, little ones, close your eyes so tight,
For the Whispers come, in the dead of night.
But fear not their call, for the dawn will soon rise,
Chasing away the dark, and their haunting cries.

As Pettie sang, the shadowy figures began to retreat, disappearing back into the fog from whence they came. The oppressive atmosphere began to lift, and the room slowly returned to normal. But the sense of relief was short-lived.

Virginia, tears streaming down her face, picked up the discarded locket. "It should have been me. It should have been me for her. That's what they said. Me for her! Oh Grant! What have I done? Pettie, my darling!"

Like a drowning man I clutched at my family holding them to my chest. Virginia sobbed, Alan was as mute as Pettie now, but at least his skin wasn't cold. My daughter was freezing, as cold as the grave.

No! I can't think like that! I can't believe that! I glanced down at my daughter but the upturned face that studied me held no hope.

And I knew the truth...Pettie was already gone.

She'd never really come back.

I was holding a stranger.

Chapter Eleven—Alan

The parlor's dimly lit interior was a stark contrast to the unsettling darkness that enveloped the rest of Laurel House. Flickering lamp light cast eerie, dancing shadows on the walls, and the crackling of the fireplace was the only sound breaking the heavy silence.

The plush blanket beneath me felt soft, almost comforting, yet the atmosphere was thick with tension. I curled up on the sofa tugging the blanket around my shoulders. It was cold in this room, despite the fire. But then again, it was cold in every room of this house. I hated this house. So strange since I'd loved it when I first arrived. Laurel House had been a place of wonder.

Now? Now, it was a place of nightmares. Mother cried all the time. Father talked to himself, or to his ghost friend, Quincy. And Pettie wasn't herself. What did that make me? Crazy too?

I nestled deeper into the makeshift bed on the sofa, trying to make a comfortable spot amidst the cushions and blankets. Pettie was to my right, her face serene in slumber, her chest rising and falling rhythmically. Her body was cold, but I didn't want her to leave. As much as I was afraid of her, I loved her.

She was my little sister, still.

My parents were huddled together on the opposite sofa, their shared look of concern evident even in the dim light. The events of the night weighed heavily on all of us. Exhaustion slowly overtook my anxiety, and I felt my eyelids grow heavy. As I drifted into slumber, the boundary between reality and dreams began to blur.

Suddenly, I was no longer in the safety of the parlor but standing at the edge of a vast, fog-shrouded field. No. Not a field. It was muddy. Yes, muddy beneath my bare feet.

The ground beneath me was cold and damp, the air thick with a foreboding mist. The moon, blood-red, hung low in the sky, casting an eerie glow that barely penetrated the fog.

From the depths of the mist, I heard soft, melodic whispers. At first, they were indistinguishable, but as they grew louder and more persistent, I realized they were calling my name.

"Alan... Alan... Join us..."

A chill ran down my spine. The whispers were not just voices; they were luring me, pulling me deeper into the moor. I did not want to obey them but something inside me would not allow me to say no. I tried to resist the whispers, to turn back, but my feet moved on their own, each step drawing me closer to the source of the voices.

As I ventured further, shadowy figures began to emerge from the fog.

Children! Their faces pale and eyes hollow, stood in a circle, their hands joined. They chanted in unison, their voices forming the haunting melody of the Midnight Veil. At the center of the circle, a dark vortex swirled, its pull almost magnetic.

Oh no! They didn't want to be here either, but their feet would not let them leave. They were captured. Was I captured too?

I tried to scream, to call out for help, but no sound escaped my lips. The children's chants grew louder, drowning out every other sound. Their hollow eyes fixed on me, filled with a sorrow that seemed centuries old.

Suddenly, a hand gripped my arm, pulling me back with a force that nearly toppled me.

I turned to see Pettie, her face contorted with fear. "Don't listen to them, Alan," she cried, her voice filled with desperation. "They want to trap you, like they did to me!"

"Pettie? I knew you could speak! I heard you singing that night. Why are we here?"

But even as she spoke, the vortex's pull grew stronger, and the ground beneath us began to give way. We were being sucked in, the world around us spinning in a dizzying whirl of colors and sounds. Pettie screamed beside me. She called my name again and again.

"Alan! Don't let me go!" Her scream was long and heartbreaking. I tasted dirt in my mouth. Was I going to be buried alive? I kicked and swung until I was fully awake.

Yes, I'd been sleeping. I woke up, the parlor's familiar surroundings rushing back into focus. My heart raced, the nightmare's terror still fresh in my mind. The dream had felt so real, so vivid, that for a moment, I struggled to separate it from reality.

But as I glanced around, trying to calm my racing heart, I realized something was amiss. The parlor was just as I'd left it, with one glaring exception—Pettie's spot beside me was empty.

The emptiness beside me was a void that sent a fresh wave of terror coursing through my veins. The soft indentation on the cushion was the only testament to her presence mere moments ago.

Panic surged, and I shot up, scanning the room desperately for any sign of Pettie.

"Pettie! Where are you?"

"Mother? Father?" My voice quivered, barely rising above a whisper. But to my horror, they remained in their deep slumber, undisturbed by my distress. Their faces, pale in the dim light, looked almost ethereal, making the room feel like a frozen tableau of time.

The Whispers had returned, their haunting lullaby more pronounced, curling around me like a cold mist.

Only I wasn't sleeping. No, this was no nightmare. Their voices were no longer just in my dreams; they were here, in the parlor, drawing me in with their insidious pull.

"Pettie..." I murmured, my voice breaking. The weight of her absence, combined with the oppressive atmosphere, threatened to suffocate me.

Every shadow in the room seemed to pulse with a malevolent energy, every flicker of the candlelight casting grotesque shapes that danced on the walls.

I took a shaky step towards the parlor door, the polished wooden floor cold beneath my bare feet. The Whispers grew louder, more urgent, their voices intertwining in a symphony of dread.

"Alan... Come to us... Find her...She is with us!"

With a trembling hand, I reached for the door handle, its cold metal sending shivers up my arm. As I slowly pushed the door open, a draft of cold air rushed in, making the candles flicker wildly. The corridor beyond was shrouded in darkness, the only light emanating from the distant glow of the moon filtering through the windows.

Taking a deep, steadying breath, I stepped out, the corridor's oppressive silence amplifying the rapid beat of my heart.

The Whispers seemed to come from everywhere and nowhere, guiding me, luring me deeper into the bowels of Laurel House.

I followed their call, each step echoing ominously in the vast emptiness of the mansion. As I moved, faint silhouettes darted in and out of my peripheral vision, always just out of reach, their fleeting forms a testament to the house's haunting history.

"Pettie!" I called out, my voice echoing back at me, distorted and unfamiliar. But there was no response, only the ever-present Whispers, their voices rising and falling like the tide.

A soft, melodic tune reached my ears, its haunting notes familiar yet chilling. It was Pettie's lullaby, the one she often hummed when she was scared or upset. The sound seemed to emanate from the garden, drawing me towards it with an irresistible force.

How was I in the garden again? How did I get here?

As I neared the entrance to the garden, the moonlight revealed a heart-wrenching sight.

Pettie, stood at the edge of the sacrificial site, her back to me, humming her lullaby with a voice filled with sorrow.

Tears welled up in my eyes as I called out to her, "Pettie! It's me, Alan! Please come back!"

But as I reached out to her, a strong hand gripped my shoulder, pulling me back with a force that made me stumble. I turned to see my father, his face a mask of fear and determination.

"We need to get her out of there," he whispered, his gaze fixed on my sister. "But we need to be careful, Alan."

"Are we awake, Father?" I asked quietly, but he did not answer. I had no idea what was happening. I didn't understand any of this. And as we stood there, on the precipice of the unknown, the weight of our family's dark legacy pressed down on us, threatening to consume us whole.

Father's grip on my arm was tight, almost painfully so, but it anchored me to reality amidst the chaos of the garden. The once serene haven was now transformed, its beauty distorted by the haunting presence of the Midnight Veil.

The gnarled trees that had once stood as silent sentinels now seemed to writhe and twist, their branches elongating into grotesque shapes, as if trying to ensnare us in their grasp. The very air was thick with anticipation, charged with an energy that made the hair on the back of my neck stand on end.

Pettie was mere steps away from the white stone slab, but the distance felt insurmountable. Her silhouette, illuminated by the ghostly moonlight, stood rigid, her voice rising and falling in a melancholic cadence.

The lullaby she hummed was a beacon, drawing me in, urging me to join her.

"Father, we have to get her!" I whispered, desperation evident in my voice.

He nodded, his jaw set with determination. "We will, son. On my count," he murmured, "we move together. Stay close to me, Alan." The Whispers swirled around us, their voices growing more frantic, their message clear: they didn't want us to reach Pettie. As we took our first tentative steps, the ground beneath us seemed to shift, the grassy path becoming treacherous and uneven.

Every shadow, every rustling leaf held a new threat. Phantom shapes flitted in and out of my peripheral vision, their ethereal forms dancing just out of reach. The very fabric of reality seemed to warp, the boundaries between the past and the present, the living and the dead, becoming increasingly blurred.

"Father, look!" I gasped, pointing towards a shimmering shadow that had materialized in front of Pettie.

Its surface rippled like water, and within its depths, I could see fleeting images of sorrow and despair—faces of those lost to the Midnight Veil, their expressions etched with eternal pain.

Children! So many children!

Pettie's voice grew louder, her lullaby now interspersed with sobs. She reached out, her fingers mere inches from the shadow, her intent clear. She was about to touch it.

"No!" Father shouted, lunging forward, pulling me along with him. We moved as one, our combined force breaking through the oppressive atmosphere.

Just as Pettie's fingers were about to contact the shadow, Father reached out, pulling her back into a tight embrace. The garden erupted into chaos.

The Whispers howled in fury, their voices reaching a deafening pitch. The very ground trembled, and the trees swayed violently, as if caught in a tempest. At the center of it all was the sound of a beast, a strong, angry beast. It growled at us in a language no living human would understand. Of that, I was sure.

But amidst the turmoil, a bubble of calm enveloped us.

Pettie, still sobbing, clung to Father. I joined them, wrapping my arms around them both, drawing strength from our collective resolve.

"We won't let them take you, Pettie," Father murmured, his voice filled with a fierce determination. "We're together."

As his words echoed in the stillness, the Whispers began to recede, their voices fading into the distance, leaving us in the heart of the garden, united in our resolve to confront the dark legacy of Laurel House.

The feeling of unity was short-lived. The growling continued and I could hear footsteps pounding on the ground.

Father, clutching both Pettie and me tightly, stood defiantly, his eyes darting around, looking for an escape route. But the garden had transformed into an impenetrable maze, the paths twisted and turned upon themselves, and the once familiar landmarks were obscured by a dense fog that rolled in, seemingly out of nowhere.

From the fog, ethereal figures began to emerge—lost souls ensnared by the Midnight Veil. Their faces, contorted with anguish, reached out to us, their whispers now plaintive cries for release.

"Stay close to me," Father urged, his voice barely audible over the cacophony of wails. But his words were more for himself than for us. The weight of our family's history, the responsibility to free these tormented souls, bore down on him.

As we navigated the garden, the figures grew bolder, trying to pull us into their sorrowful embrace. Each touch, cold and lifeless, drained our energy, our hope. Pettie, her strength waning, collapsed and my father picked her up.

Suddenly, a familiar face emerged from the mist—Mother!

"Me for her," she rasped, her voice echoing with despair, "We cannot run. You cannot run."

Father halted; his gaze locked with Mother's. "Virginia! What are you doing? I have Pettie! Let's go, Virginia! Please, listen to me."

But before any words could be exchanged, a powerful force pulled Mother back and into the fog that collected behind her, her outstretched arms reaching for Father, her voice a fading whisper.

"Save them, Grant... Set us free..."

"No! Virginia! Don't leave! Don't go with them!" With renewed determination, Father tightened his grip on us.

"Father?" I asked fearfully. He was holding Pettie, she wasn't moving. She looked like a sack of flour laid across his shoulder. He clutched my hand.

"Come, Alan! Stay with me. Don't let go!" As we continued our desperate escape, the garden began to change. The fog lifted, revealing the sacrificial site ahead. A stone altar, bathed in the moonlight, stood as a beacon, drawing us closer.

With every step towards the altar, the Whispers grew silent, the spectral figures receding into the shadows. The oppressive weight of the garden's malevolence began to lift, replaced by an almost palpable anticipation.

But then I began to shake. I shook so hard I woke myself up. My eyes snapped open, the chilling remnants of the nightmare still clinging to me. The dim, muted light of the parlor greeted me, and the comforting silhouettes of my parents resting nearby.

Father's even breathing and the gentle rise and fall of Mother's chest indicated they were still lost in sleep. But the empty space beside me, where Pettie had been sleeping, was a stark contrast to the tranquil scene.

Panic welled up inside me. "Pettie?" I whispered, hoping she was merely hidden beneath the blankets or had shifted to the floor. But there was no response, no movement. The weight of her absence pressed down on me like a heavy shroud.

I struggled to my feet, the eerie silence of the house amplifying my growing anxiety. How could she vanish, again, without a sound? Without waking any of us?

"Pettie?" I called out again, my voice echoing back at me. No response. A sinking feeling settled in my stomach. The house, in its eerie stillness, felt alive, listening, waiting.

Mother woke first. She knew immediately what had happened. They got her, the dark ones. The Midnight Veil had come and taken her and we'd all been dreaming about it.

All of us.

And somehow, we'd lost Pettie again.

Chapter Twelve–Virginia

The morning light that usually streamed through the drapes of Laurel House was strangely absent, replaced by a dim, melancholic grayness. I awoke with a start, my heart still racing from the remnants of a nightmare I couldn't quite remember.

As I sat up, the weight of recent events pressed down on me—the loss of Mrs. Higgins, Pettie's mysterious second disappearance, and the oppressive history of my husband's family's legacy.

Pulling the blankets tighter around me, I tried to dispel the unease that had settled deep in my bones. The grand halls of Laurel House, which had once echoed with laughter and warmth, now seemed cold and foreboding.

I had so much hope for this place when we first arrived. We were going to have a second chance. A second chance for all of us. The silence was almost palpable, broken only by the distant ticking of the grandfather clock in the hallway.

I slipped out of bed, my bare feet touching the cold wooden floor. The absence of Mrs. Higgins was felt acutely. What did the remainder of the staff think about her being missing? No one came to me to formally turn in their notice but I knew many of my house staff had left. Their usual morning routines—the soft hum of conversation, the clinking of dishes, the smell of breakfast cooking—were all conspicuously much quieter. The house felt hollow, as if it too mourned the losses.

Moving to the window, I gently pulled aside the curtain, hoping to catch a glimpse of the outside world. But the view that greeted me was one of gloom. Thick, heavy clouds blanketed the sky, their oppressive presence echoing the heaviness in my heart.

Trying to shake off the feeling of impending doom, I reached for Evelyn's letter on the bedside table. Her words had been a beacon of hope in these trying times.

As I unfolded the papers, I took a deep breath, hoping to find some help in her written words but really, what help could there be? The minister had run from the house, his clothes practically on fire. He would not return, his curt tone made that clear.

Who was left to help guide us out of the darkness and to the light? Grant should have told me about this place! He should have warned me, but he said nothing. Now it was too late.

With Evelyn's letter clutched tightly in hand, I moved to the ornate writing desk that had been in my family for generations. It felt surreal, sitting here, surrounded by the weight of my husband's family history, and the curse that had ensnared us all.

The very air felt thick, as if the walls of Laurel House held within them the whispered secrets of the past.

I took out my personal stationery and pen, preparing to write a response.

Grant had insisted on traveling to town to report Pettie's sudden disappearance. He had wanted me to accompany him, but the thought of leaving Laurel House, even for a brief moment, filled me with an inexplicable dread.

What if Pettie returned and found us gone?

And so, with a heavy heart, I had watched him leave, Alan's small hand held tightly in his.

The quiet scratching of my pen on paper was almost therapeutic. With each word, I poured out my anxieties, my fears, and my hopes to Evelyn.

My sister, Evelyn was smart. A woman who could solve the intricacies of the Sullivan family history and help lift the weight of the curse that loomed over us.

Surely all would be well! All would be well!

But as I wrote, a cold breeze swept through the room, making the curtains flutter wildly. I paused, my hand hovering above the paper. The windows were securely shut, and yet, the room had suddenly turned cold.

My heart began to race as I realized that I was no longer alone. A soft whisper, barely audible, seemed to come from above.

The attic.

I placed the pen down slowly, my senses on high alert. The whispers grew louder, more insistent. With trepidation, I rose from the desk, compelled to investigate the source of the eerie sound. Taking a deep breath, I prepared myself for what lay ahead.

The grand staircase leading to the attic had always given me a sense of foreboding. I rarely traveled up here. With each creak of the wooden stairs beneath my feet, the whispers grew louder, drawing me closer to the attic's entrance.

The door stood slightly ajar, an inviting yet ominous gap that seemed to beckon me forward. I hesitated for a moment, the weight of anticipation pressing down on my chest. The dim light from below barely penetrated the attic's darkness, casting eerie shadows on the walls.

Taking a deep breath, I pushed the door open further. The whispers intensified, now a cacophony of voices, each vying for my attention. But amidst the chaos, one voice stood out—a child's voice, plaintive and familiar.

"Hello?" I whispered, my voice trembling with a mixture of hope and fear. "Pettie? Honey, is that you?"

As my eyes adjusted to the dimness, I noticed a small, rocking chair in the corner, its gentle movement casting flickering shadows. And there, in the chair, was the faint silhouette of a child, her back turned to me.

I approached slowly, every instinct urging caution. "Pettie, sweetheart?" I asked, my voice barely above a whisper. Every inch of my body told me to run but I couldn't. What if it was truly my little daughter?

The figure in the chair remained still, the only sound being the soft creaking of the rocking chair and the ever-present whispers that seemed to emanate from the very walls of the attic.

The shadows seemed to dance and twirl around the room, playing tricks on my eyes. I reached out, my fingers just inches from the child's shoulder, the weight of uncertainty pressing down on me. "Pettie?" I murmured once more, my voice thick with emotion.

As I made contact, the figure turned to face me. But it wasn't Pettie.

Instead, a ghostly apparition of her stared back, her eyes hollow and devoid of life, her face twisted in an expression of eternal sorrow. A chill ran down my spine as the realization hit me—this was not my daughter, but a spirit, a remnant of the past.

The apparition's lips moved, and though no sound came out, the words formed were clear.

Help me, Mother.

"You're not Pettie." I stumbled back, my heart racing. The whispers intensified, their voices mocking, taunting. Every corner of the attic seemed to come alive, the darkness pulsating with malevolent energy. "Pettie!" I cried out, desperate to find my real daughter amidst this nightmare. But the ghostly figure only continued to stare, its gaze piercing through me, a silent plea for release.

The weight of Grant's family history, the curse that had plagued generations, became palpable. The spirits of Laurel House were restless, and I was caught in their web of sorrow and despair.

Why, Grant! You should have told me!

Gasping for breath, I backed away from the apparition, my mind racing for a way out. But the more I retreated, the more the shadows closed in, the whispers growing louder, more insistent.

The oppressive weight of the attic became unbearable. The Whispers grew in volume and intensity, their voices no longer distinguishable from one another, merging into a cacophonous symphony of anguish and torment. The very air around me seemed to grow dense, and the room dimmed as if a thick, black veil had been drawn across it.

Each step I took felt as if I were wading through a quagmire, the ground beneath my feet seeming to give way with every movement. Panic welled up inside me, a primal fear taking hold as I felt the malevolent spirits close in, their presence tangible, oppressive.

"Give me my daughter! Pettie! Pettie! I'm here!"

In a last-ditch attempt to free myself from this ensnaring darkness, I reached for the attic's window, hoping to let in a glimmer of the outside world. But my hand met only cold, unyielding glass.

The Whispers seemed to mock my futile efforts, their laughter echoing eerily in the confined space.

Shadows began to manifest, forming dark, undulating masses that moved with a life of their own. They reached out, their cold, wispy fingers grazing my skin, sending shivers down my spine. The temperature in the attic plummeted, and I could see my breath, each exhale forming a misty cloud in the frosty air. For some reason, I found it hard to breathe and began to cough.

I felt trapped, ensnared by these malevolent entities. Were they going to smother me?

Their grip on me tightened, and it became increasingly difficult to breathe. My vision blurred, the room spinning as I felt myself being pulled into the abyss of despair that the Whispers had created.

Desperation took hold, and I screamed, my voice echoing in the vast emptiness of the attic. But the Whispers only grew louder, drowning out my cries for help, their malevolence palpable as they reveled in my terror.

Barely able to stand, my legs gave way, and I stumbled back, crashing into a forgotten trunk filled with age-old relics of my husband's family past. The impact sent a cloud of dust into the air, momentarily obscuring my vision.

As the haze settled, I heard the distant rumble of thunder outside, a storm that mirrored the tempestuous events unfolding within the confines of Laurel House.

Outside! I'm going to have to go outside!

Desperate to escape the attic's suffocating grasp, I turned my gaze to the only exit—a narrow, creaky staircase that seemed miles away.

Mustering every ounce of strength I had left, I made a dash for it, the Whispers' icy fingers brushing against my skin, attempting to pull me back.

"No!" I screamed in protest to their unwanted touching.

The world outside the window transformed before my eyes. The once-clear skies were now darkened with ominous clouds, and a torrential downpour began, each raindrop sounding like a heavy drumbeat, amplifying the sense of impending doom.

The garden, once a sanctuary of tranquility, now appeared as a twisted labyrinth of shadows and despair. The vibrant flora had turned dark and wilted, seemingly mourning the events that had transpired. But it wasn't just the storm or the transformed garden that filled me with dread; it was the fog.

A thick, impenetrable fog rolled in, enveloping everything in its path, reducing visibility to mere inches. It was as if the Midnight Veil itself had descended upon the world outside, blurring the boundaries between the living and the dead.

I hesitated at the window, the chilling realization setting in. There was no escape. Not from this house, not from its curse, and certainly not from the relentless Whispers that seemed to have taken a sinister delight in my torment.

The Whispers grew louder, more insistent, their voices merging into a singular, haunting chant. *You for her. You for her.* It felt as though the very walls of Laurel House were reciting the mantra, echoing the sentiment back at me with a chilling resonance.

Every step I took was heavier than the last, my feet sinking into the plush carpet as if being pulled downward by unseen hands. The air grew colder, and every breath I took tasted of metallic bitterness. The oppressive weight of my husband's family's history and the curse became palpable, pressing down on me from all sides. It was as if the house itself wanted to claim me.

My heart raced, its beats echoing the rhythm of the chant. The realization hit me with a force that nearly knocked the wind out of me.

They wanted a trade. A life for a life. My life in exchange for Pettie's freedom.

The weight of that understanding bore down on me, and I found myself sinking to my knees, tears streaming down my face. But amidst the despair, a defiant spark ignited within me.

If I really believed that Pettie would return, I would have granted their wish, but who could trust such evil. I did not. My Pettie was stolen from me and whatever had returned had been only a shell, a cruel mockery of the child I loved so completely.

Gathering my strength, I rose to my feet, ready to confront the Whispers and whatever dark force had ensnared my family. I refused to be trapped within the walls of this cursed mansion, and I wouldn't go down without a fight.

My husband needed me! Alan needed his mother! And Pettie...my poor little girl!

My legs pounded as I raced down the stairs and made it to the front door. The world outside was a stark contrast to the oppressive atmosphere within Laurel House.

The skies had turned an eerie shade of dark gray, as if twilight had descended prematurely. The looming trees swayed wildly, their leaves rustling and branches groaning as if lamenting an impending doom.

The garden, once a haven of beauty and solace, had transformed into a foreboding labyrinth. The fog, thick and suffocating, obscured the path ahead, reducing visibility to mere feet. Yet, even in this dense mist, I could feel the eyes upon me, watching, waiting.

I stepped onto the gravel path, the familiar crunching sound offering a small semblance of normality. But as I ventured deeper into the garden, the path seemed to shift and change, leading me further into unknown territory. The haunting chant of the Whispers seemed to come from all directions now.

You for her. You for her.

A chilling wind whipped around me, sending shivers down my spine and tangling my hair. Despite the fear threatening to paralyze me, I pressed on, driven by a mother's desperation and a fierce determination to break free from this nightmare.

Suddenly, from the shadows of the garden, figures began to emerge. Not just the ethereal souls trapped by the Midnight Veil, but shadowy, shapeless entities that seemed to be born from the very darkness itself. They circled around me, their movements fluid and menacing, closing in.

I felt a pang of desperation, a gnawing realization that perhaps I had walked straight into a trap. But surrendering to despair wasn't an option.

Taking a deep breath, I prepared to face whatever lay ahead, clutching the letter from Evelyn as if it were a lifeline.

My footsteps became frantic, the gravel crunching loudly beneath my feet as I tried to evade the encroaching shadows. Each breath I took was labored, the cold, damp air of the garden filling my lungs. But the Whispers seemed to grow even louder, the repeated chant of *YOU FOR HER* echoing endlessly in my ears.

A particularly thick tendril of shadow reached out, grazing my arm. The cold touch sent an electric jolt through me, and the world began to spin. I stumbled, barely managing to keep my footing, but the shadows were relentless.

In the midst of the chaos, a heart-wrenching scream pierced the air. It was my scream, a sound of raw terror and desperation. The shadows had ensnared me, their icy grip tightening with every passing second.

I felt the weight of my husband's family's legacy pressing down, the sins of the past demanding retribution.

The garden, once a symbol of life and growth, would become my prison, the very earth and air conspiring against me. I could feel the life being drained from me, the shadows feeding on my fear and despair. And then, just as suddenly as it had started, everything fell silent. The garden was plunged into darkness, the only sound my ragged breathing and the faint, distant Whispers that seemed to taunt me.

The silence was almost more terrifying than the cacophony that had preceded it.

Every part of me was on high alert, listening intently for any sign, any whisper that would indicate what was to come next. The weight of the darkness was oppressive, smothering, as if the very air had been sucked out of the garden.

My heartbeat, loud and erratic, was the only indication that time was still passing. The shadows had released their vice-like grip, but I could feel them lurking just beyond my vision, waiting, watching.

A cold gust of wind swept through the garden, and I wrapped my arms around myself, trying to ward off the chill that had nothing to do with the temperature. I felt exposed, vulnerable, knowing that I was at the mercy of forces far beyond my comprehension.

Slowly, almost imperceptibly, a dim light began to filter through the trees. The source of the illumination was not the comforting glow of the sun but rather a sickly, pale luminescence that painted everything in an eerie, otherworldly hue. It was as if the garden had been transported to another realm, one where the rules of reality no longer applied.

As the light grew stronger, I could make out the swirling forms of the Whispers, their ethereal shapes twisting and writhing in a macabre dance. The repeated chant of YOU FOR HER was now more insistent, more demanding.

I knew, deep in my bones, that the end was near. The Whispers would not be denied their sacrifice.

Tears stung my eyes, not just from fear but from the grief of all I was leaving behind.

My husband, my children, the life we had built together – all seemed to be slipping away from me. And yet, amidst the darkness and the haunting chants, a clarity began to take hold in my mind.

Maybe it was true. Maybe I could take her place? How could I say no then?

If sacrificing myself was the key to saving Pettie, to saving my family, then I would willingly embrace that fate.

Drawing upon a reservoir of courage I didn't know I possessed, I took a deep breath and stepped forward, closer to the swirling mass of Whispers. Their movements became more frenzied, their voices rising in a crescendo of anticipation.

"Take me," I whispered, my voice trembling, but resolute. "Take me and release my daughter."

For a moment, there was a hushed silence, as if the very world was holding its breath.

And then, in a rush of wind and shadow, the Whispers converged upon me, their cold, ethereal fingers reaching out to claim their screaming prize.

"Grant!" Was the last thing on my tongue, but it wouldn't be enough to save me.

Nobody would be saved.

Chapter Thirteen—Grant

I pushed open the front door, expecting to see my wife's lovely face greeting me; I'd been anxious about leaving her alone but she insisted I go report Pettie's second disappearance.

The door creaked on its hinges, an ominous sound that filled the empty house like a sigh from some forgotten ghost. The silence that met me was deafening, a void that spoke volumes. Without warning, a strange sick feeling gripped me.

"Virginia? Are you upstairs?" I called out expectantly but there was no reply. A chill raced down my spine. Alan was immediately by my side, his small hand in mine. Poor child. I barely knew how to comfort him.

We moved from room to room, each one echoing the emptiness of the last. Her absence hung in the air, a palpable thing, heavy and suffocating. I felt like I was drowning, submerged in a sea of dread and disbelief.

"I think she might've gone for a walk," I replied, attempting a tone of casual assurance that I didn't feel.

Alan looked puzzled, his young eyes squinting in confusion. "In the garden? Why would she go there? Father, she shouldn't go there!" My throat tightened; the reality of his observation struck like a hammer. What if she had gone into the garden?

I knelt down, leveling my eyes with his, trying to shield him from the terror that was beginning to gnaw at me. "I'm sure she's fine. Maybe she needed some fresh air. Don't worry, I'll find her and bring her back. And Pettie too." I hugged him close, his small body trembling against mine. I felt his uncertainty, his fear, and it fueled my own.

Where had she gone? And why did it feel like the life we had known had just shattered into a million unrecognizable pieces?

After searching the house and the grounds, as far as I could dare to go, we went back to Laurel House.

I made Alan a plate of cold cheese, ham and bread and told him to stay in the dining room. I needed a moment to collect my thoughts and possibly pound my first against a wall.

I found myself standing in the study, my fingers skimming over old books and dusty papers, anything that might hold an answer. As I looked through my own father's collection of journals and letters, a fragment of a conversation I had with Quincy bubbled up in my mind.

Yes, I'd had a conversation with a ghost! Quincy was a ghost! Was there any help for us?

The magistrate looked at me as if I'd committed some sort of crime when I reported my daughter's most recent disappearance. Of course, what else would they think? And now, with Virginia missing...

Quincy had hinted at a forbidden ritual, something passed down in our family but never openly discussed or described in detail. The conversation with Quincy hadn't been the only mention of this I'd heard before. I suddenly recalled that I'd overheard Father, Quincy and Mother whispering about strange signs and rituals.

I wasn't supposed to be listening, but I was quite good at eavesdropping. You had to be with my father or else you would know nothing at all. I felt a twinge of hope, then a heavier feeling of desperation.

What was this ritual? Could it be the key to undoing the curse? And if so, why had father never elaborated on it?

My head spun as I dug deeper into his writings, scanning for any inkling of this hidden knowledge. In the middle of my frenzied search, Alan walked in. "Father, I'm finished with supper. I don't want to be alone anymore."

I looked at him, his face full of fear and his expression gnawed at me. "You don't have to be alone, son. Stay with me. Help me sort this mess. Let's stack it all up."

"What are you looking for, Father?"

I sighed and tousled his hair with my hand. I wanted to pull him close and weep, but that wouldn't help the situation.

"I'm not sure. Maybe your mother left a note and forgot to leave it where we could find it." It wasn't an unreasonable guess, but certainly unlikely. But something must have been leading me, because I quickly spotted the letter, the one from Evelyn.

As I read her words, it became increasingly clear that she possessed more than a little esoteric knowledge. Her letter touched on spiritual realms and ancient practices in a way that seemed almost scholarly, yet deeply personal. Could she know something about the forbidden ritual Quincy had hinted at?

I didn't really know my sister-in-law and had never met my brother-in-law.

Without wasting another second, I grabbed a pen and paper. My fingers flew across the page as I wrote to her, spilling out my desperation and the terrible urgency of the situation.

"Dear Evelyn, I have bad news to share. Things here have not gone well. My dear wife, your sister, she and our little Pettie are missing," I continued to write furiously. *"I have reason to believe that an old family curse is involved, and I desperately need your guidance. I see that my wife has written you already. I regret that I did not take her fears as seriously as necessary, but now, Evelyn...if you and Donald could make your way here, I should be eternally grateful. Please come quickly!"*

I sealed the letter, feeling a cocktail of hope and dread churn inside me. I told myself I'd done all I could for the night. It was a small comfort, but a necessary one. I put the letter in the post the same day. I had to continue my search for Virginia, but the day was speeding back, and the darkness was descending.

Alan and I made another trip around the house, but there was no evidence of my wife's coming or going since the last time we checked.

With no servants around and no one to help me, I decided Alan and I would ride to town again tomorrow morning, first thing.

Something was going on here, the magistrate couldn't ignore both Pettie and Virginia's disappearance.

My son and I spent the night huddled together in his bedroom; a chair tucked under the doorknob to prevent anyone from breaking in. Would that be enough? Could a chair keep the ghosts out? As expected, the Whispers returned, frantic, frenetic voices demanding my attention.

At least Alan was asleep. At least he couldn't hear them. I closed my eyes tightly to prevent the tears from flowing. Once they started, I could not guarantee I could stop them, and my son didn't need to see his father crying.

Grant...come outside. Grant, come find me. And just like that, the Whispers took on my wife's soft voice. Clearly to torment me. *Grant, please...*

As night inched closer to day, the voices faded away and I could finally close my eyes. It was like that every day. Day upon day. Alan and I spent our days searching for Pettie and Virginia, but we found nothing at all. The magistrate came by once and made his way around, he even brought two deputies with him but they, too, found nothing.

Not a trace of Virginia and Pettie Sullivan.

Days rolled by like fog, thick and indistinct, as I waited for Evelyn's response to my letter.

I buried myself in the study, surrounded by a maze of old books and arcane artifacts. Alan stayed with me, bless the boy. He made sure we had snacks to eat as he helped me pull books and find clues about the Midnight Veil.

A knock at the front door startled me out of my trance. I made Alan hide behind the door as I went to answer it.

When I opened it, there stood the Reverend, the very same who had run away when we'd needed his help before. He looked chastened, his eyes bearing the weight of unspoken regret.

"Hear me out, sir. I apologize for not assisting you earlier, Mr. Sullivan," he began hesitantly, "I was afraid, and that's no excuse. I behaved shamefully, but I would like to talk with you. Is your wife home? I think I have found a way to help all of you."

I looked at him, my eyes narrowed. "Your apologies won't help me," I said, my voice icy and tinged with bitterness. "It's best you leave. If you stay, you'll only get hurt."

Rev. Thomas nodded solemnly but then lifted his gaze to meet mine. "You won't hear me out at least? Wait! Is something wrong with Mrs. Sullivan? What has happened, sir?"

How dare he demand answers from me! I couldn't believe it!

"She's gone along with my daughter. If you have said all that you needed to say, I'd like to close my door. Goodbye, reverend. Please don't come back."

"Please, Mr. Sullivan. I'll leave for now, but I would like to come back tomorrow. Whether you like it or not, you need all the help you can get, and I intend to offer mine."

"We've had enough of your help!" I shouted at him as I slammed the door in his face. Fool of a man! I had closed the door without another word, but his promise—or perhaps it was a warning—lingered in the air.

As I returned to my study, with Alan in tow, my thoughts swirled with doubt and anticipation. I felt as if I were wading through an endless swamp of despair. I plunked down behind my desk and my son put his arms around me. We held one another for a moment when another knock resonated through the house.

Could this be the minister again? He'd not left but five minutes ago.

"What now?" I opened the door furiously, and found Evelyn, just as I remembered her, only this time accompanied by a man I assumed was her husband.

"Grant? Not a minute too late, I see. You look as if you haven't slept in a week," she said, as if reading my most urgent thoughts. "Virginia's letter was... quite compelling. Where is she?" She put her bag down on the floor beside the door as her husband walked in behind her.

Relief and despair washed over me. "Please, come inside. Let me help you with your bags. Alan, help you Aunt Evelyn—and Donald, is it?"

"Yes, this is my husband Donald. Oh, thank you, Alan. Look how big you've grown. Tell me, where is Virginia?"

"Son, help Uncle Donald take the bags to the upstairs guest room. Take him to the room next to yours but come right back." Alan studied my face for a moment but asked no question.

As Alan and Donald moved Evelyn's bags into the living room, I leaned closer to my sister-in-law. "Virginia is missing, along with Pettie. That's why I wrote to you," I whispered, trying to keep the distress out of my voice. "I guess you haven't had time to receive my letter. You're here because of Evelyn's letter."

Evelyn's face paled. "Missing? What exactly do you mean, Grant? Where did you last see Virginia and Pettie."

"The garden took Pettie. I'm not sure about Virginia. I can't imagine she would have gone out there without me, unless as Alan suggests they lured her out. The Whispers."

"Oh, Grant, you should have sent someone! We need to understand—"

Just then, a loud crash echoed from the study, cutting her off. We all turned toward the noise, hearts pounding. Donald and Alan raced back, alarmed. "What was that—"

Before he could finish his sentence, the lights in the house flickered and went out, plunging us into darkness.

A chilling whisper seemed to float through the air, saying, "Too late."

The chilling silence was suddenly broken by deliberate, haunting footsteps echoing from the study. Each step seemed to be weighed down with intent, growing louder and more ominous as they approached through the suffocating darkness. In the midst of this void, a faint, eerie hum began to permeate the air. It was the haunting tune of a lullaby; one Virginia would tenderly sing to Alan. But this time, it was twisted, dripping with malevolence.

The room grew dense with a palpable dread. Every shadow seemed to writhe and contort, as if alive. Whatever unspeakable entity had invaded our sanctuary was now merely a whisper away.

I instinctively clutched Alan close, my pulse racing, every ounce of my being screaming for escape as we braced for what might come next.

Chapter Fourteen—Grant

The old wooden floorboards creaked ominously beneath our feet as we made our way towards the source of the unsettling sound. The house was shrouded in a silence so thick, it felt like wading through a dense fog.

Every tick of the ancient grandfather clock seemed to reverberate through the corridor, punctuating the eerie stillness. I could hear my own heartbeat echoing loudly in my ears, and I was sure the others could too. I imagined my son's heart was pounding noisily too. I squeezed his hand to assure him that I'd protect him.

I prayed that I could.

As we ascended the narrow staircase leading to the attic, I felt a cold draft snake its way around my ankles and up my spine, causing me to shiver involuntarily. The rickety steps groaned under our combined weight, and every fiber of my being screamed at me to turn back. But my curiosity, or perhaps my foolhardiness, propelled me forward.

Pushing open the creaky attic door, a sight met our eyes that made the hairs on the back of my neck stand on end. A once neatly packed trunk lay overturned, its contents strewn haphazardly all over the floor. Old letters, photographs, and trinkets from a bygone era littered the space. The dim light filtering in from the small attic window caught the glint of something metallic. An old locket, perhaps? That looked so familiar.

Evelyn, her face pale and her eyes wide, looked around the room, her gaze distant and unfocused.

After what felt like an eternity, she finally spoke, her voice trembling, "The spirits... they're trying to tell us something." She gingerly picked up a faded photograph from the ground, her fingers trembling. "They want us to find the answers. The truth lies here, Grant. It is somewhere amidst these memories."

I looked at her, then at the disarray around us. The weight of countless secrets seemed to press down on the room, and I had an unnerving feeling that we were not alone in our quest for answers. Whatever had happened in this old house, the remnants of the past were crying out to be heard. And we were about to uncover them.

The dim light from the attic window cast long, eerie shadows that danced upon the wooden floor. As I sifted through the scattered remnants of the past, my fingers brushed against the cool, rough texture of worn leather.

Pulling it from the jumble, I realized I was holding an old journal, its surface marred by time and use, with the leather cracked and peeling in places.

I opened it carefully, the spine protesting with a soft creak. The pages were brittle and yellowed, the edges frayed from countless hands that had once turned them. The ink, once a deep, rich black, had now faded to a dull brown. But what caught my attention were the dates.

The entries spanned decades, some even hinting at being centuries old. How could a journal last so long, and who had written in it?

Compelled by an inexplicable urge, I began to read an entry out loud. The words, though written in an elegant, looping script, seemed to squirm on the page, morphing and shifting as I tried to make them out. It was as if they were alive, resisting being read, or perhaps changing their narrative. "This is weird. It's like the words are moving."

"Try again," Evelyn encouraged me quietly. Donald had his arm around her shoulder, but his eyes were large with wonder.

I took a deep breath and began to read the text again.

"After midnight becomes darkest, and the moon veils her face, and the winds whisper secrets of the forgotten," I began, my voice echoing slightly in the stillness of the attic. But as I continued, the words began to twist and turn, reshaping themselves, "He will come, the witness of dark secrets, for he watches from the shadows, waiting for the moment to reclaim what was once his."

A chill ran down my spine, and I abruptly closed the journal, my heart racing. Nobody said anything but at least the banging and whispers had stopped.

The atmosphere in the attic felt even more oppressive, the weight of unseen eyes pressing down on us. The journal, it seemed, held more than just old memories. It was a gateway to the past, and perhaps to something much darker.

The attic was filled with the musty scent of old wood and aged paper as I continued to read from the journal. But as the words flowed from my lips, I noticed a change in Evelyn. A slight change at first but the longer I watched her, the longer I read from the journal, the more she quieted. Yes, she was quite affected by what was going on.

Her usually sharp and observant eyes took on a distant, glazed look. Her body swayed slightly, like a willow tree caught in a gentle breeze, and her voice began to murmur words that were disjointed and incomprehensible.

The attic was thick with tension as I continued reading, the weight of old memories pressing down on us.

"Evelyn?" I whispered, a hint of concern in my voice. But she seemed miles away, trapped in another time and place. Around me, the others shifted uneasily, their faces masks of confusion and worry.

Donald, ever the voice of reason, whispered to me, "Don't interrupt her, Grant. She's channeling something. Stay quiet, and she might reveal what she's seeing."

For what felt like an eternity, we watched in silence as Evelyn mumbled phrases, her voice a soft, eerie whisper. "The children... ghostly figures in the hallway... they play but can't find rest." Her face contorted in distress. "Whispers... so many whispers... souls taken too soon, seeking release."

The air grew colder, and a shiver ran down my spine as I tried to make sense of her words.

And then, as if waking from a deep sleep, Evelyn's trance broke. Her eyes, now clear but filled with a mixture of awe and terror, darted around the room, taking in each of us. She inhaled sharply, her chest rising and falling rapidly.

"It's all connected," she whispered, her voice shaky. "The stories, the souls, this house. We're not alone here. I saw it," she whispered, her voice trembling. "A vision of the past, as clear as day."

We gathered around her, waiting for her to continue. She took a moment to collect herself, then began to speak.

"It was night, and the house was alive with the sounds of a grand ball. Music, laughter, the clinking of glasses. But in a hidden corner of this very attic, two figures met in secret. A young woman, dressed in a gown of the purest white, and a man in a sharp suit. Their love was forbidden, kept hidden from prying eyes. Their stolen moments were filled with whispered promises and tender touches."

Evelyn paused, her eyes clouding with sadness. "But their love was not meant to be. I saw them being discovered, the fury in the eyes of those who found them. The young woman was dragged away, her cries echoing through the halls. The man, in his desperation, met a tragic end. They were the first. They had a plan, an awful plan, but they were not successful. Not in life. Only in death. "

She took a deep breath, her eyes glistening with unshed tears. "This house holds secrets, memories of love and loss."

The room was silent, the weight of Evelyn's vision pressing down on us. The past had come alive, and we were caught in its grip.

"He was your great grandfather, Grant. They killed them both, your great grandfather and his lover, they were the founders of the Midnight Veil. He killed your grandmother. I heard him thinking about it. It was a lucky spin of the Wheel of Fortune they were stopped, but others came. Their followers continued their dark practices. The curse they created was powered with their own deaths and they've gotten stronger. They've soaked the graves of children and the innocent. They are all trapped and have no choice but to serve their masters. We must set them free. If we can do that, we can save Virginia and Pettie. It may not be too late for them."

Nobody said a word, but I nodded to show I'd heard and listened. The attic, once silent save for our footsteps and murmured conversations, began to change. An icy coldness permeated the air, sending goosebumps racing across our exposed skin. It felt as if the very walls were exhaling cold breaths, wrapping us in a frigid embrace. I pulled my jacket tighter around me, trying to ward off the creeping cold.

Then came the whispers.

At first, they were faint, like the rustling of old newspapers or the distant murmur of a conversation. But as we continued our search, the whispers grew louder, more insistent. They echoed around us, coming from all directions, making it impossible to pinpoint their source.

Words and phrases intertwined, creating a cacophony of hushed voices, all desperate to be heard.

Donald strained his ears, trying to decipher the words. "Do you hear that?" he asked, his voice barely above a whisper itself. "It sounds like... voices. Many voices."

Evelyn nodded, her eyes wide. "It's them. The stolen souls. They're trying to communicate with us."

I turned my gaze to the walls, where the dim light from our torches cast long, dancing shadows. But these weren't ordinary shadows. They writhed and shifted, coalescing into humanoid shapes that flitted across the wooden panels. Faces without features, arms reaching out, only to dissolve back into the darkness.

Alan, clutching my hand, but with his free hand pointed towards a particularly dark corner. "Look there!" he exclaimed. A group of shadowy figures seemed to huddle together, their outlines wavering as if they were made of smoke. They moved in unison, swaying to a rhythm only they could hear.

We stood still, entranced by the spectacle before us. The attic, with its forgotten memories and lingering souls, had come alive, and we were in the heart of its mystery. The dim, cold atmosphere of the attic was interrupted by a gleam, a faint shimmer that caught my eye.

Nestled amidst the scattered remnants of the trunk, lay a familiar locket. Its silver chain tangled with old letters and fabric, the pendant half-buried beneath yellowed photographs. "How did this get up here?" I reached out hesitantly, the weight of memories heavy in the air. It was the same locket that once belonged to my mother, the very one I'd entrusted to Virginia.

As I held the locket, its cold metal warming to my touch, I felt an odd sensation, like a current of electricity coursing through my veins. The locket pulsed with an energy; a force that seemed almost alive.

Donald, always the skeptic, reached out, curiosity evident in his eyes. "May I?" he asked, fingers already outstretched. I handed it to him, watching his expression closely. As his fingers closed around the pendant, his eyes widened, and he jerked back slightly, as if he'd been stung.

"It's charged with power," he murmured, eyes locked onto the gleaming pendant. "Even I can feel it, and I'm no medium. This isn't just a keepsake, Grant. It's a conduit. Somehow, this locket is connected to the Midnight Veil."

The room seemed to grow even colder, the shadows deeper.

The locket, once a symbol of love and family, now held a more sinister significance. The whispers grew louder, and the dancing shadows more frantic, as if the locket's revelation stirred them. Whatever secrets it held, they were now intertwined with our fates.

Without a word of warning, Evelyn reached out with her embroidered handkerchief and covered the locket. Using the cloth to protect her skin, she examined it. "Yes, it's charged, Donald. You gave this to Virginia? Couldn't you tell something was wrong?"

"No. It was my mother's necklace. She wore it all the time. What?"

Donald put his hand on his wife's shoulder. "I think we should try to rest. We're safe for tonight. I'll make sure of that, but we do need to rest. Tomorrow is the new moon. That's when we'll confront the spirits in the house, and the garden. Don't worry, Grant. We'll find them."

I thanked him and together Alan and I went to the master bedroom. A thousand things went through my mind as my son and I went through the motions of getting ready for bed.

How was Donald going to "make sure" we were safe tonight? I'd love to know, but I was too tired to ask. He was right, I needed the rest. I needed food too, but I was too tired to prepare anything. If Alan had asked, I would have scrounged around the pantry for something, but he didn't, so I didn't bring it up. I tucked my son in on Virginia's side of the bed and I lay down beside him. From my vantage point I could see the door and the broken mirror that hung on the wall.

Something inside me warned me. I rose from the bed quietly and covered the mirror with my wife's shawl. Breathing a sigh of relief, I fell asleep quickly. I hadn't expected it, but I welcomed the rest. I woke up once or twice to make sure Alan was safe beside me. He didn't move either.

After a few hours, I lay in the dark and silently prayed to a God who barely knew me.

I received no assurances, but hoped that he heard me, because even I knew that tomorrow's confrontation would be a journey into darkness.

One I hoped we all returned from.

Chapter Fifteen—Evelyn

"The doorway must be in the garden," I declared, my eyes locking onto Grant's with an intensity that seared through the room. "That's where this all began and where it must end." I shoved a basket of bread in front of him, along with some cold butter. I'd barely slept, but Donald had been correct. Grant and Alan needed normalcy, for what we were about to do battle with would shake their souls.

"Thank you," Alan said as he reached for a slice of bread. I was glad that my husband had insisted that we bring food. I would never have imagined that we'd need it, but my husband was an intuitive man, for all his claims to be a strict scientist.

Even I knew that wasn't completely true. It couldn't be. Not anymore. Donald and I had been traveling the East Coast. The college had sent him on a speaking tour, the subject of which was spiritualism and its effects on our culture. Along the way, we'd heard a lot of stories and visited a lot of so-called haunted or vexed places.

"What's the plan for today?" Grant asked as he sat beside Alan and watched him eat a few bites.

"We go to the garden. We must, Grant. I need to see the place, look for traces of ritual practice."

He sighed visibly and agreed. "I know exactly what you're talking about. There is a place that was probably used for their purposes. Quincy showed it to me."

"I'd like to talk to him. Is he close by?"

Alan glanced up at his father waiting for his answer. What was going on between them? What was it about Quincy that stirred such fear? "Grant?"

"When I was a lad, Quincy worked for my father, here at Laurel House. He was the gardener, but he was more than that. He was kind and my parents considered him a friend. The day I returned, or somewhere near that, I met Quincy in the garden. I had no idea that anything was wrong. I suppose I should have known what he was, what he'd become, but I was so glad to see him. I had forgotten so much about my childhood, but Quincy, he helped me. Then when Pettie disappeared... He was there."

"He was a spirit, wasn't he? Quincy was a ghost." Grant's eyes met mine. He didn't say a word, but he didn't have to. I sat beside him, my heart broke for him. He clearly had never had to deal with anything like this before. Neither had I, not this close to my own family, but we were here now.

"It sounds to me like Quincy was trying to help you. We could use his help, I think. Let's go to the garden. Show us what you've found. We'll find a way to make contact with Quincy again. Maybe he can give us clues as to where to find Virginia and Pettie." I said hopefully, but I wasn't actually that hopeful. I suspected that my sister and niece had been taken to a place that there was no return from.

A knock on the door startled me. Donald and I followed Alan to the hallway to see who the visitor might be. Alan was beside me. I reached out to put my hand on his shoulder, but he pulled away.

Poor child. This had forever changed him.

"Reverend Thomas, I thought I'd made myself clear yesterday. We don't need your help." Grant kept his hand on the doorknob, but I hurried to his side. My brother-in-law didn't fight me. He allowed me to open the door and welcome the guest. I was surprised to see he wasn't alone.

"Reverend Thomas, is it? My name is Evelyn and this is my husband, Professor Donald Phelps. We're here to help Grant. Why are you here, sir?"

The reverend, who had walked in the room, his voice steeped in guilt and worry, finally broke his silence. "As I told Mr. Sullivan yesterday, I'll do whatever is necessary to help. I am sorry that I failed to protect him. Go, do what you must. I'll keep watch over Alan," he offered, his voice tinged with a regret so palpable it was as if he was trying to atone for all his past failures with this single act. "These good men and women are members of my church. They will pray for your success," he promised as he waved his hand at the black clad gathering. "I assume you'll be continuing the search for Mrs. Sullivan and your young daughter?"

That question was for Grant who quickly agreed. "Yes, that's right. I don't want you to get hurt, Reverend. You or your church members. Perhaps you should go, sir."

I studied the odd collective. Why were they dressed for a funeral? That didn't seem appropriate in the current situation. My sister and niece were missing, not dead.

One of the women in the group rose and stood beside Alan. She had a smile on her face, but I still shivered. Her strange cryptic smile didn't quite reach her eyes. What did I see there? Something I didn't like.

"We will pray down the heavens for them, Mr. Sullivan. Let us help you how we can."

Grant's eyes wavered, caught in a tumultuous dance between me, the reverend, his son, and the door that served as a gateway to the peony garden. We had no time to waste. A fact that my husband quietly reminded him.

"Right. Let's do this. Alan, remain inside the house with Reverend Thomas," Grant finally said, his voice a mix of reluctant acceptance and encroaching dread. With those words, we stepped over an invisible threshold, leaving behind the semblance of a normal world and plunging into one woven from shadows and whispered secrets.

"Father..." he began to argue with Grant, but he raised his hand. I watched as he pulled him close and hugged him. He whispered in his son's ear. "Stay here and watch over things. Please, stay inside the house. No matter what."

"Okay, Father. I will stay here but promise me you'll come back." Grant woodenly promised and the three of us headed outside.

"We'll be praying from here," Reverend Thomas assured us and as if on cue, his gathering rose to their feet and nodded their assent. A few immediately clasped their hands and began praying.

The three of us stepped in unison into the frigid embrace of the day, a palpable tension binding us together like the threads of some dark tapestry.

Above us, the sky was a vault of impenetrable black, as though the heavens themselves had turned away, unwilling to bear witness to the grim tableau that was about to unfold. An electric current of anticipation charged the air, prickling the skin and raising the fine hairs on the nape of my neck.

With every step toward the accursed peony garden, the gravel pathway crunched underfoot, each stone breaking like fragile skeletal remains beneath our weight.

"We must find the right grave. There should be something, some kind of marker," Donald murmured to himself. Poor Donald. It was always strange to see him outside the classroom. Normally, he taught on these matters, he wasn't one to work in the actual field, or take on a case personally. Yes, I loved him, even if he wasn't the man of my dreams. There were worse things to be than married to a boring man.

At least he had a good heart and was intelligent. And he was willing to help me rescue Virginia and Pettie.

My sister and I had not been friends in years. Not like we used to be. I wasn't exactly sure why, but the point was moot now. I would forgive everything if I could find her and bring her back home.

The night seemed to absorb the sound of our footfalls, enveloping us in a stifling silence as oppressive as a burial shroud. An anemic moon strained to pierce the thick curtain of clouds, its feeble light casting grotesque shadows that contorted on the earth beneath us, writhing and twisting as though tormented by invisible demons.

The garden loomed ahead, its once vibrant colors now a palette of murky greys and ghostly whites. The beauty it once held was marred, twisted into something ominous. It felt as though we were walking into the maw of some great beast, willing, yet wary, of the dark depths that awaited us.

As we stepped into the garden's confines, the air itself seemed to grow dense with an unspeakable tension, as though nature was holding its collective breath in anxious dread.

"It may be here," Grant guided us to a remote corner, a hidden recess far removed from the judgmental gaze of the house and the world that lay beyond its walls. It was here that a series of modest, anonymous graves rested, like vile secrets murmured in the depths of the night.

"One of these is a gateway. I can feel it, Donald," I breathed out, my voice trembling between awe and trepidation.

My eyes moved hesitantly across the graves, each mound a puzzle of earthly layers—similar, yet uniquely different, as if each were the gnarled fingerprint of the departed soul it sheltered. "But which one? Oh no. These poor souls, little children. All of them."

The atmosphere congealed around us, becoming almost palpable, a cold, wet mist as if the very soil exuded a clammy, nervous sweat.

Each grave seemed to emit both a magnetic pull and a repellent force—a complex tangle of allure and warning. An owl's sorrowful hoot pierced the heavy quietude from some distant perch, its haunting cry lingering in the air like a ghostly dirge. The ground beneath us felt as though it were alive, its subtle vibrations seeming to await our decision—or ominously, to make the decision for us.

Scarcely had we shifted our focus to the enigmatic graves when a cacophony of unnerving whispers infiltrated the air, slithering through the night like smoky tendrils on a malevolent breeze.

"Evelyn, come closer. We must stay together." Donald reached for me and I raced to him.

They escalated, a crescendo of murmured voices that felt as though they emerged from both the very bowels of the earth and the twisted limbs that sprawled menacingly above us.

"We're not alone," Donald declared, his timbre saturated with a disquieting epiphany. His gaze flickered feverishly, scouring the labyrinthine interplay of shadows and half-light that lay between each solemn tombstone.

"I want my wife and daughter, you bastards! Give me Virginia and Pettie!" Grant shouted into the blackness.

In a chilling response, the whispers seemed to evolve, their formless utterances condensing into fragmented words I couldn't decipher—a haunting syntax woven from desolation and yearning, an inscrutable tongue spoken only by the forsaken.

"Look, Donald!" I pointed to the garden's periphery; shadows began to meld and intensify, aggregating into forms of deeper, impenetrable darkness. They wavered and elongated as if probing the limits of their own corporeal reality before lunging at us with the ferocity of famished beasts.

We had been ensnared, lured into a diabolical snare meticulously woven by the ghostly inhabitants of this damned hellscape. Lured by a volatile cocktail of desperate optimism and inescapable need, we were now the hunted in a most malevolent game.

As the shadows surged forward in their sinister advance, a visceral surge of raw survivalism erupted within me.

"Run!" I shrieked, my voice cleaving through the dense, suffocating silence like a blade.

Our feet drummed violently against the frigid soil as we sprinted, each inhalation slicing our lungs, each exhalation a shallow pant of terror.

The shadows morphed, stretching into malevolent tendrils yearning to ensnare us in an abyss of eternal darkness. Lacking physical form, yet brimming with nefarious intent, they closed in like a nightmarish tide. Every stride we took was like trudging through a quagmire of invisible resistance, as if the cursed earth itself sought to shackle us.

Hot tears stung my eyes, smearing my vision into a chaotic blur.

Even so, I glimpsed Grant's silhouette darting ahead—a fleeting wraith propelled by raw desperation. Behind me, Donald murmured esoteric incantations, words culled from the musty pages of forgotten tomes, a fragile bulwark against the encroaching malevolence that swirled like a tempest around us.

We burst into a clearing, a meager oasis awash in the sickly luminescence of a moon that seemed almost reluctant to shed its light upon us. Huddled, gasping for air, shivering in the aftermath of adrenaline, we locked eyes and braced ourselves.

For a heartbeat, the shadows, too, hesitated, their amorphous darkness rippling at the fringes of this fragile sanctuary. It was a loaded pause, a ceasefire in a conflict too cryptic for any of us to fully comprehend.

It was in that haunting lull that an icy realization impaled me: this enigmatic garden, with its clandestine graves and murmured myths, had yet to unveil its most maleficent mysteries.

I felt a curious heft in my pocket and recalled the small vial of salt I'd carried—a vestige of superstitions too deep-rooted to ignore. Shaking hands hastily removed the cork, scattering a protective circle of salt around our quivering forms.

"Precautions," I breathed out, locking eyes with Grant. His nod was tinged with a complex cocktail of dread and gratitude, as if acknowledging both the terror of the moment and the small comfort that the salt I sprinkled into our pockets offered. The pause snapped. Provoked or enraged by our feeble ritual, the whispers swelled into a cacophonous dirge.

The shadows at the fringes of our ephemeral sanctuary began to seethe and roil, their formless contours swirling into a tempest of palpable malevolence.

It was as if the darkness itself had been personally affronted by our feeble salt, provoked into a frothing rage that belied their lack of corporeal form. They pulsed and quivered, a churning mass of unadulterated darkness eager to unleash their pent-up fury.

And then, with a venomous surge of otherworldly malice, they lunged.

The fragile standoff we'd managed to establish splintered like glass under a hammer's blow, the eerie stillness shattered by their renewed assault. A cacophony of incoherent shrieks and growls filled the air, a discordant symphony of despair and rage that tore through the night like a hurricane through reeds.

These weren't just absences of light; they were voracious voids, anti-beings that sought to consume all that was good and pure. As they broke the barrier, their elongated tendrils whipped toward us, oozing an acrid stench of rot and decay.

It was as if the very air had soured in their presence, growing thick with the noxious fumes of a thousand damned souls. They stretched towards us like the fingers of a giant spectral hand, reaching to clutch us into an embrace of eternal darkness.

For a moment, it felt as if the world had paused, time stretching taut as a wire. Every fiber of my being screamed to flee, to escape this nightmarish tableau, but we stood paralyzed, our eyes transfixed on the oncoming abyss.

It was a moment of perfect, horrifying clarity, when all illusions were stripped away, leaving only the raw, pulsating dread of the incomprehensible.

The instant they transgressed our personal space, the shadows recoiled, unleashing a chorus of torturous wails that reverberated through the air, a discordant symphony of rage and torment. The salt was our frail, yet vital, bulwark against an onslaught that otherwise seemed inexorable.

Our eyes locked in a fleeting triangulation of tenuous relief and simmering dread. No words were exchanged; the air was too laden with the brittle tension of a moment that could shatter at any second. The salty perimeter might have held, but we were far from free, ensnared still in a garden that breathed malevolence from its very soil.

An instinctive whisper in my gut said our torturous trials were nowhere near their end.

Within that gossamer bubble of safety, our eyes entwined in a complex dance of hope and trepidation. A visceral tug in the depths of my being yanked my gaze toward a singular grave, unobtrusive in its appearance, yet inexplicably compelling. It was an odd magnetism, a pull that felt simultaneously inviting and repulsive.

"That one," I murmured, my arm quivering as it breached the protective salt circle to point at the enigmatic mound of earth. "That's it. This is where they first invoked their magic. Where they first made contact. This is where they stole the first soul, Grant."

Grant's eyes flickered between me and the indicated grave, then offered a subtle nod of assent.

It was an old grave, the stone worn and broken, but I could feel the power and I could feel what lurked beneath it.

Donald had quickly abandoned his normal position as the cynic. Doubt was a luxury we could ill afford; our predicament was too perilously balanced on the knife-edge of despair.

The moment was shattered as a wail ripped through the garden, different from the whispers or the shadows. It was a cry of anguish, full of sorrow and despair, echoing from the very bowels of the earth.

Oh no! Was that Alan? It sounded like a male child!

My heart dropped, a heavy stone sinking into a sea of dread. It was a sound no living being should ever have to hear, and it promised nothing but agony.

"It is trying to trick us. It wants us to quit! We need to move, and we need to move now," Grant said, his voice laced with a new urgency.

I nodded, clutching the vial of salt tightly in my hand. Whatever lay ahead, our path was fraught with peril. But standing still was no longer an option.

Taking a deep breath, I stepped over the line of salt, immediately feeling the air grow colder, denser, as if filled with the weight of unseen eyes. Grant and the Donald followed, casting wary glances back at the retreating sanctuary of our makeshift circle.

We made our way to the grave I had pointed out, each step feeling like a mile, each second stretching on like an eternity.

My heartbeat pounded in my ears, a frenetic drum drowning out the distant whispers and soft rustling of the leaves.

As we reached the grave, I felt a nauseating swirl of energies, like currents in a dark, bottomless ocean. Yes, this was the place. This unassuming patch of earth was a gateway to something far beyond our understanding.

"We don't have much time," I said, my voice catching in my throat. "Whatever we're going to do, we have to do it now."

Grant looked at the grave and then back at me, his eyes filled with a mixture of resolve and apprehension. The Professor stood a little farther back, clutching an old leather-bound book—his face pale, but set.

I knew then that we were committed to this harrowing journey, wherever it would lead. The dread that enveloped us was palpable, a living entity of its own. But despite it, or maybe because of it, I felt a surge of grim determination.

We would face whatever horrors awaited us on the other side of that grave. There was simply no turning back.

The tension in the air thickened to an almost suffocating degree, each of us hyper-aware of the other, as if the slightest movement could trigger an avalanche of unknown horrors.

"Stand back," Grant warned, removing from his pocket the locket and pendant that he'd given his wife.

Just as he knelt by the grave, a bone-chilling howl pierced the stillness, and the ground beneath us trembled as if angered by our audacity.

Shadows at the edges of the garden twisted and writhed, morphing into grotesque shapes that defied description. And I felt it—the presence. Not just watching, but staring through us, as if it could glimpse our very souls.

The necklace dangled from his hand. It was clear what he planned to do. He was going to open the portal with the power of the necklace and locket. Was this a good idea? What was going to happen? I couldn't be sure. None of us could. The theory was once the door was open we would see Virginia and Pettie. As they'd entered the other dimension alive, there was a chance that they were still among the living, but there was no time to wait.

"Grant," the Professor stammered, "do it quickly! Hang the necklace on the stone. Evelyn, quickly! Bring the bag!"

Suddenly, the ground before us erupted as an unseen force seemed to push up from beneath the grave, scattering soil and small pebbles. The atmosphere was electric, charged with an energy that was malevolent and intoxicating all at once. I felt both repulsed and strangely drawn to it, a dichotomy that shook me to my core.

"Give me back my wife and daughter! I command you!" Grant shouted as he backed away from the ancient grave marker.

Time seemed to freeze; the silence so profound it was almost a physical force. Then, the whispers returned, but now they were different, elated, victorious. It was as if we had passed some unspoken test, or perhaps more troublingly, sealed some unspoken pact.

Just then, a gust of wind swept through the garden, and for a brief moment, I felt an overwhelming sensation of being pulled in two opposite directions—torn between realms.

I stumbled back, heart pounding, as a voice broke through the whispers—a voice so achingly familiar, it seized my soul. *Sister! I hear you!*

It was Virginia's voice, but it was twisted, as if her voice were coming through a veil of water or glass. Distorted, but unmistakably her.

"Evelyn... help..."

The voice trailed off into an indistinct murmur, swallowed by a cacophony of other voices, each more tortured than the last. I felt my knees weaken, but I fought the urge to collapse.

"Give me the dagger, Donald," I whispered as I reached out my hand.

"Dagger? What are you doing?" Grant demanded, but I ignored him. There wasn't enough time to explain to him how I would use the dagger, or why we needed it. There simply wasn't time.

Then, without warning, the locket and pendant levitated, glowing with an otherworldly light. For a split second, a blinding flare shot forth from it, illuminating the faces of Grant, the Professor, and me in an eerie, spectral glow.

Just as abruptly, they plummeted back to the grave, sinking into the disturbed earth like a stone in water, swallowed whole by the enigmatic force we had unwittingly unleashed.

"Did it—did it work?" the Professor stammered, his eyes wide with a mix of fear and wonder. "Did we open the portal? We need to find Virginia and Pettie. They should be close to the entrance."

Before any of us could respond, the soil of the grave started to ripple, as if something—or someone—was about to break through from the other side. The whispers swelled into a frenzied chant, their cadence unsettlingly celebratory.

Suddenly, a hand burst through the soil, its fingers skeletal and elongated, scrabbling at the air as if seeking something—or someone—to grasp. It was followed by another, and another, skeletal hands reaching up as if beckoned by an invisible conductor. I watched in terror as they reached for me.

Aghast, I tried to back away, my eyes locked onto the shadowy forms emerging from the bluish light behind the grave marker. It was pitch black outside and appeared poised to rain down thunder and lightning on us all.

What had we done?

I screamed against the tugs of the dried husks of hands. Grant, pale as death, tugged at me and helped me get free.

And as we stood there, our backs against the inky blackness, surrounded by the unholy chorus of whispering voices and the grotesque hands reaching for us from the earth, we realized we were standing at the threshold of an abyss, peering into a realm of nightmares.

And then, just as quickly as they had appeared, the hands withdrew back into the grave, the soil settling as if nothing had happened.

But the whispers continued, more malevolent than ever. And somewhere in the distance, beyond the garden, beyond the veil of reality we understood, a guttural laugh resonated—ominous, satisfied, and infinitely terrifying.

"Ready or not," the voice boomed from the depths, echoing through the very marrow of our bones, "here I come."

The air grew deathly still. We exchanged glances, our faces etched with terror and disbelief, knowing that we had just opened a door that could never be closed.

A door to an abyss that now knew our names.

Chapter Sixteen—Alan

The wooden front door creaked shut behind my father, leaving me alone in that room. My heart raced, each beat echoing the dread that welled up inside me. Before I could even process my father's absence, the reverend, towering and imposing, closed the distance between us.

His firm hands grabbed my shoulders, shoving me into an ornate wooden chair. Leaning in, his cold breath grazed my ear. "Stay put," he whispered, the threat evident in his tone.

Father!

I attempted to meet the ministers' eyes, searching for some hint of mercy, but the intensity I found made me quickly avert my gaze. Some of the women removed black candles from their purses and popped matches to light them. The dim candlelight threw eerie, stretching shadows against the walls, heightening my unease.

Father! Please come back!

I felt the congregation's eyes on me, their stares heavy and unrelenting. I was trapped, their focus suffocating me, and I knew in that moment that I was ensnared in something far more sinister than I'd ever imagined. I couldn't think of what to do, say, or how to defend myself. In the end, I did nothing.

I tried to steady my breathing, to keep my rising panic in check, but the room shifted into an even more chilling atmosphere.

Members of the congregation, their faces now obscured by hooded cloaks, began to form a tight circle around the room's center. Their postures were almost ritualistic, heads bowed low as they fell to their knees, their hands raised upwards in a pleading gesture.

Then, it began.

A chant. Soft at first, like a distant echo, but it quickly grew in intensity, filling the room with an otherworldly resonance. The melodies they chanted were unfamiliar to me, the words in a language I couldn't recognize. I didn't like it. I didn't like this at all. And to think, just a few weeks ago, we'd sang hymns with these same souls. Now I was seeing them for who they truly were—evil workers!

Even though I was terrified, their collective chant was haunting, hypnotic.

Their eyes, previously fixed on me, now rolled back, showing only the whites, as if they were in a trance. The energy in the room became palpable, the very air seemed to vibrate with the force of their voices.

A realization hit me with chilling clarity: this was no ordinary church gathering.

I was in the presence of the Midnight Veil, the shadowy cult I'd only heard whispers of in hushed conversations. What had happened to Pettie and Mother, this was their fault!

The weight of this truth bore down on me, the room's walls feeling like they were closing in. It was a sensation of overwhelming dread, and the urge to escape grew stronger with every passing second.

With the congregation lost in their eerie trance, I saw my chance to run. My heart pounded loudly in my ears, each beat urging me to move, to flee. The exit was clear, but I didn't dare head for the door. Instead, I bolted for the staircase, my small feet pounding against the wooden steps. The echo of my hasty retreat seemed deafening, but the congregation continued their chant, oblivious to my escape.

Reaching the top, I glanced over my shoulder, half-expecting someone to be in pursuit. But to my surprise, the path behind me was empty. The haunting melodies still drifted upwards, but no one had broken away to chase me. The realization was both a relief and a mystery.

Why weren't they coming after me? Didn't they know I was gone?

I didn't dwell on it for long. The urge to hide, to find a safe haven, was too overpowering. I darted into the nearest room, closing the door softly behind me.

My breathing was erratic, my small frame shaking from the adrenaline.

I pressed my ear against the door, listening intently. The chanting persisted, but there was no sound of footsteps, no indication that they were aware of my escape. For now, I was safe, but I knew I couldn't let my guard down.

Not while in the heart of the Midnight Veil's lair.

Time seemed to stretch endlessly as I remained hidden in my sanctuary. But as the minutes passed, a growing commotion from outside began to pull at my curiosity. Muffled shouts, the clashing of what sounded like weapons, and an energy that felt both electric and otherworldly.

Tentatively, I approached the window, my fingertips lightly grazing the cool glass pane. The garden below was awash with chaos. Figures moved rapidly, shadows darting and weaving, their forms almost blending into the night. The garden, once a place of solace and beauty, was now transformed into a battleground of dark forces. As I continued to watch the chaos unfold, a sudden gust of wind brushed past me, ruffling the curtains and sending a chill down my spine. But with that wind came something else – a whisper, faint, but unmistakable.

"Alan..."

It was a voice, or perhaps multiple voices, layered and intertwined. My heart raced as recognition dawned. The soft cadence of my mother, the playful lilt of my sister. They were calling out to me, their voices distant, yet strangely comforting.

I closed my eyes for a moment, trying to focus on the sounds, to trace them to their source. The garden battle raged on, but those ethereal voices seemed to exist in a space all their own, separate from the turmoil below.

"Alan... We're here..."

The words seemed to float around me, enveloping me in a warm embrace. The connection was palpable, a lifeline in the midst of the storm. It was as if they were reaching out, trying to bridge the gap between our worlds.

Tears welled up in my eyes. Despite the chaos, despite the fear, I felt their presence—Mother and Pettie. I wasn't alone. The bond we shared was unbreakable, and in that moment, I clung to it with all my might.

The once familiar walls of the house seemed to close in on me as the ritual downstairs intensified. The haunting chants grew louder, more fervent, echoing through the corridors and seeping into every crevice.

I could feel the energy, a pulsating force that resonated with every beat of my heart.

They'll come for me soon, Pettie! They'll get me too!

I tried to block the chants out, pressing my hands against my ears, but it was inescapable. The very air around me vibrated with power, and a pressure built inside my head, making it hard to think.

Images flashed before my eyes—twisted faces, shadows moving in the periphery, and blinding lights.

Emotions washed over me in waves: fear, sadness, longing, and a deep sense of loss. It was as if I was experiencing a myriad of lifetimes all at once, memories that weren't my own.

What was this? What was I experiencing?

Suddenly, the weight of it all became too much. My legs gave way, and I collapsed onto the floor, gasping for breath. But even as darkness threatened to consume me, I could hear them—the members of the Midnight Veil—ascending the stairs, their footsteps methodical and deliberate.

"Alan..." they whispered, their voices intertwining in a sinister lullaby.

As the world around me blurred, I could feel the presence of the Midnight Veil drawing nearer, the fear palpable. The last thing I remembered before succumbing to the overwhelming sensations was the cold touch of a hand on my forehead and the realization that they had finally found me.

But the darkness that had enveloped me shifted, morphing into a dreamlike landscape that seemed both familiar and alien. I was no longer in the attic.

I was outside and away from the horrible chanting.

The ground beneath my feet was soft, like walking on a bed of moss, and the sky above shimmered with hues of purples and blues, casting an ethereal glow on everything. I was outside, but not outside. Of this world, but not of this world. Turning slightly, I saw Mother and Pettie, standing a short distance away, bathed in a soft luminescence.

"Alan, darling," Mother called, her voice soft and melodic, echoing in the stillness. She looked just as I remembered—kind, gentle, with that maternal warmth that always made me feel safe.

Pettie's eyes sparkled with mischief, just as they always had.

I rushed to them, tears forming in my eyes. The reunion was brief, but the emotions were intense. We hugged and I never wanted to let them go, but we could not remain in this state. Amidst the joy, there was an underlying sadness—a sense of finality.

Mother took my face in her hands, her gaze piercing into mine. "Watch your sister, Alan," she whispered, her voice filled with pride. "I love you, my son."

"No, Mother! Don't leave me! Please, don't go, Mother," I wept as she slid from my hands. As our moment together began to fade, a large, collective shadow loomed in the distance, signaling the encroaching presence of the Midnight Veil.

I felt a tug at my heart, pulling me back to reality.

But as the dream dissolved, their words of encouragement lingered, giving me the strength to face whatever awaited me next. The serenity of my brief reunion with Mother and Pettie was abruptly shattered as the shadow from the far horizon surged forward, transforming the dreamscape around me.

The soft mossy ground gave way to hard, cold stone, and I found myself in a vast graveyard, cloaked in an oppressive fog.

Tombstones, old and weathered, rose around me like silent sentinels, their inscriptions worn away by time. The eerie stillness was broken only by the sound of my own heartbeat, thundering in my ears.

A cold wind whispered through the gravestones, carrying with it the haunting chants of the Midnight Veil.

"Pettie!" I called out, my voice desperate. "Where are you? Father! It's me! Alan! Help me!"

I began to run, my footsteps echoing eerily. Every shadow seemed to move, every whisper seemed to call my name.

The members of the Midnight Veil emerged from the mist, their eyes glowing with an unnatural light, reaching out for me with long, bony fingers.

"Pettie, you must come. You must. Mother told me to watch over you," I sobbed in the gloomy fog.

A soft touch on my cheek pulled me from the depths of my sorrow.

My eyes fluttered open, adjusting to the fog around me. For a moment, the lines between dream and reality blurred, and I half expected to see the ominous members of the Midnight Veil looming over me. But instead, I was met with the comforting sight of my sister's young face.

"Alan," she whispered, her voice gentle and soothing. "There you are." I blinked, trying to process everything. The chilling chase through the graveyard, the echoing voices, the terror—it all felt so real. "Stay down, Alan. Don't let them see you. Be quiet and very still."

My sister gently pushed me down, her fingers brushing the hair from my forehead. "Quiet," she urged. "Or they'll find us."

I nodded weakly, closing my eyes for a moment, praying that this was real. That Pettie was real and she wasn't going to leave me.

That would have to be enough for now.

Chapter Seventeen—Grant

I moved toward the edge of the garden, the ground beneath me feeling less like soil and more like a minefield of dread and wonder. The air was thick, reality itself seemed to warp, making the trees and the flowers look like twisted caricatures of their former selves.

And there they were—Alan and Pettie locked in an embrace. My heart swelled, a strange mix of relief and disbelief coursing through me. Was it real? Could it be? The tension in my body eased ever so slightly as I reached them.

"Thank God you're safe," I murmured, hugging Pettie as if I might anchor myself to reality by the sheer force of my grip. I felt her warmth, her substance, and a wave of gratitude washed over me. I was afraid to blink, afraid that it was all a figment of desperate imagination.

Evelyn, her eyes narrowed with years of discerning the fraudulent from the genuine in the world of the supernatural, approached us cautiously. She looked Pettie over, her gaze lingering on her eyes, then her hands.

"Pettie, what's the last thing you remember before all this happened?" Evelyn's voice was tinged with a gravity that demanded truth.

Pettie looked confused for a moment, her eyes searching the ground as if it might offer her the words she needed. "I remember being in the garden. The flowers were talking to me. Mother was there too."

Evelyn sighed, the lines of tension on her face relaxing ever so slightly. "It's her. But she's not complete, Grant," she determined as she looked at me with what I could only describe as hope—something I hadn't seen in a very long time.

"What does that mean?" I reached for my daughter and pulled her close, stroking her hair. "Explain it."

"They still have a piece of her, Alan. Spirit, soul and body, that's what each of us are made of. This evil group are after the souls, her soul. They have a part of it, she's not completely free yet."

Donald interrupted her. "But she's strong and she managed to escape, so there's hope, Grant."

Evelyn's expression appeared to suggest the answer was more nuanced. I didn't want to hear what else she had to say.

No sooner had Evelyn spoken, Donald cut through the moment with an urgency that made my skin crawl. "We can't stand around analyzing. We need to close that portal, and we need to do it now! This was never meant to be opened!"

I felt a jolt of panic at his words. Even amidst the relief of having Pettie back—even if not completely—I knew he was right. The portal was an abomination, a tear in the fabric of reality that should never have existed.

Donald moved toward where the ground had been disturbed, his eyes scanning the symbols and sigils that had been hastily etched into the dirt around it. "We don't have much time. The longer it stays open, the more unstable it becomes."

"Wait!" Alan, who had been quiet, finally spoke up, his voice tinged with fear, but also a strange sort of bravery. "Dad, we need to talk. The minister, the church—it's all a part of the Midnight Veil. They're behind this."

My heart sank, a mixture of confusion and betrayal clouding my mind. How deep did this go? How tangled was the web we were caught in?

"The minister? The Midnight Veil?" The words tumbled out, clumsy and disbelieving. I was struggling to process this new, twisted layer to our nightmare.

Evelyn, her eyes widening at Alan's revelation, glanced at Donald, then back to me. "We can't close the portal yet. What about Virginia? We can't just leave her behind."

Donald paused, his eyes meeting Evelyn's. The weight of years and hard-learned lessons seemed to hang between them for a moment. "You know how this goes, Evelyn," he finally said, his voice cold, but not without a flicker of regret. "She's the sacrifice. She gave herself to set Pettie free."

The words hit me like a physical blow. I looked at Pettie, at Alan, and finally at the place where the ground had been disturbed—the portal to a realm of unknown horrors. "She gave herself?" I whispered, the words choked in my throat. "I can't accept that. I won't."

Donald's eyes narrowed, not in judgment, but perhaps in understanding. "Sometimes, we don't get to choose, Grant. Sometimes the choice is made for us."

I felt a knot tighten in my stomach, as if the very fabric of my being was rebelling against this cruel twist of fate. My eyes scanned the unsettling edge of the garden, almost expecting Virginia to emerge from the shadows, her face warm with a reassuring smile. But there was nothing; just a heavy silence that seemed to mock our despair.

Suddenly, the earth where the portal had been trembled, as if in response to our turbulent emotions. The wind picked up, and a guttural whisper wound its way through the trees, sending a shiver down my spine.

"Don't listen to it, Dad. We must close it now," Alan urged, gripping my arm with an intensity that startled me.

Evelyn started chanting something in a language I didn't understand, her voice carrying an ancient power. Donald joined in, pulling a series of small, intricately carved stones from his pocket and arranging them in a circle around the disturbed earth.

My hand shook as I reached into my pocket for the locket and pendant Virginia had always loved, knowing that using them would mean acknowledging she was gone.

But just as my fingers touched the cold metal, a piercing scream erupted from the ground, freezing us all in place. And in that terrifying moment, between the known and the unknown, I realized we weren't just closing a portal.

We were making a choice that would change our lives forever.

The scream went on and on, seeming to stretch time itself as it echoed through the trees. My heart raced as I looked at Pettie, fear etched into her features. I knew I had to act fast. Digging out the locket and pendant from my pocket, I held them up, feeling their weight in my trembling hand. I closed my eyes and let myself be enveloped in the memories they held, of Virginia's laughter and her love.

The world around me seemed to fade as I focused, feeling the energy of the talismans crackling in my palm. A sense of purpose filled me, overwhelming my fear. I opened my eyes and saw that the ground had stopped shaking, the portal now glowing ominously in the center of the circle of stones.

I moved forward, my hand outstretched, ready to perform the ritual that would close the portal once and for all. But as I approached, I saw something moving just beyond the portal's edge. It was a figure, shrouded in darkness, but its eyes glowed with an otherworldly light.

I froze, my hand hovering just inches from the locket and pendant, unsure of what to do. The figure took a step forward, then another, and suddenly I recognized her.

"Virginia!" I shouted, relief flooding me as I saw her emerge from the shadows. She was alive and unharmed, her familiar smile spreading across her face.

But as she drew closer, I saw that her eyes held a strange, almost manic gleam. Her movements were jerky, unnatural, like a marionette being pulled by unseen strings. And then, without warning, Virginia lunged at me with a speed that defied human capabilities. I stumbled backward, barely managing to avoid her grasp.

"Virginia, what's going on?" I asked, my heart pounding in my chest.

But she didn't answer. Instead, she charged at me again, her eyes blazing with a fierce intensity.

I backed away, feeling the weight of the locket and pendant in my palm. They were my only hope, the only defense I had against whatever had taken hold of Virginia.

I closed my eyes and focused, feeling the energy of the talismans pulsing through me. I opened my eyes and saw Virginia charging at me again, but this time I was ready.

With a swift motion, I held up the locket and pendant, their power radiating outwards. Virginia shrieked, her limbs flailing wildly as she recoiled from the energy of the talismans. And then, just as suddenly as it had begun, it was over. Virginia collapsed to the ground, her eyes dull and lifeless.

I rushed over to her, feeling a sense of overwhelming sadness and regret.

"I'm so sorry, Virginia," I whispered, tears streaming down my face. "I couldn't save you."

As I looked up, I saw that the portal had finally closed, the circle of stones now just a mundane arrangement of rocks in the garden. The nightmare was over, but at what cost?

I knew that we would never be the same after this, that the trauma of what we had experienced would stay with us for the rest of our lives.

But in that moment, as I cradled Virginia's lifeless body in my arms, I knew that I'd lost her and I would feel the loss forever.

The memory of Virginia's sacrifice would haunt me forever, a reminder of the weight of our choices and the cruel nature of fate.

Chapter Eighteen—Evelyn

My heart sank as I felt an unnatural shift in the air—a coldness that bit through even the warmth of the protective circle Donald had conjured. My eyes darted around the dark edges of the garden, and that's when I saw them. Shadowy figures emerging like wraiths from the mist, circling us in a slow, menacing dance. The members of The Veil Cult had arrived.

"We're not alone," I murmured, clutching Alan and Pettie closer to me. "They're here."

The cultists, their faces obscured by dark masks, stood eerily still, as if waiting for a cue to strike. I couldn't shake the feeling that we were all pawns in some otherworldly game, teetering on the edge of an abyss.

Donald's incantations still hung in the air, forming a fragile shield around us. But for how long would it hold against such malevolent forces? For the first time in years, I felt genuine fear creep into my bones, overriding all the scholarly detachment I had cultivated over the years studying the supernatural.

My gaze fell on Grant, who had dropped to his knees beside Virginia's lifeless body. He was cradling her, his hands trembling as they brushed away strands of hair from her face. It was a portrait of agony—his eyes red, awash in tears that mingled with the dust and dew on the ground beneath him.

His face was a study in contrasts: part hope, part devastation. His lips moved, whispering words I couldn't hear, but their intent was palpable—a silent prayer, a plea to whatever gods might be listening to return her to him. It was as if his very soul had been ripped from him, leaving behind a void too immense to comprehend.

For a moment, time seemed to freeze. Every cry of the night creatures, every rustle of leaves in the wind, even the air itself held its breath, as if granting him this solitary, sacred moment of grief.

Virginia lay there, an ethereal glow to her skin in the moonlight, her beauty untouched by the ordeal, yet rendered lifeless and distant. It was as though she had become a part of the dreamlike tapestry of the garden, forever disconnected from the world of the living.

The sight broke me. I gripped Alan and Pettie even tighter, my hands shaking as I tried to process the enormity of our loss. A gaping wound had been torn in our lives, one that no amount of scholarly wisdom, or arcane knowledge, could ever mend.

Donald stepped forward, his eyes meeting mine in a tacit agreement that words couldn't capture. Raising his arms, he began to chant incantations that seemed almost primal, a language that twisted the air around us, making it thicken as if attempting to fend off the malevolence that surrounded us.

A shimmering circle of light emanated from his fingertips, wrapping around us in a protective cocoon. It was a frail barrier, shimmering like gossamer, but it was enough to stem the tide of shadows encroaching on our circle.

The Veil cult that had surrounded us appeared equally confounded and entranced. Dressed in tattered robes that seemed to absorb the moonlight, they stood there, watching us with hollow eyes. Their mouths moved in eerie synchrony, whispering incantations of their own in a devilish language I couldn't recognize. It was a dissonant chorus, grating and malevolent, as if the night itself had found its voice.

My heart was pounding in my chest, each beat echoing the seconds that seemed to stretch into eternities. Clutching Pettie and Alan close to me, I felt their hearts racing in tune with my own. This was it. The moment of reckoning. The very fabric of reality seemed to quiver, as if awaiting the outcome of this cosmic showdown.

Yet, despite the arcane forces at work, despite the looming dread that painted the air with strokes of despair, it was the human element that gripped me the most: Grant's raw grief, the children's stifled fear, and Donald's quiet determination. All of it hanging in a fragile balance between hope and catastrophe.

"We have to close the portal, Alan," I said, my voice barely rising above a whisper, laced with urgency.

He looked at me, his young eyes filled with a curious blend of innocence and wisdom, as if he had glimpsed truths far beyond his years. "How, Aunt Evelyn? How can we stop this?"

I didn't have a clear answer, but there was no turning back now. Our lives, and potentially many more, hung in the balance. Forcing myself to push aside the dread clawing at the edges of my consciousness, I focused on the facts.

"The necklace and pendant. They're more than just family heirlooms. They're imbued with ancient powers that can seal the rift," I explained hurriedly. "We have to use them, and we have to do it now."

Alan's gaze shifted to his father, who was still weeping over Virginia's lifeless form. The weight of our reality, the life and death decisions thrust upon us in this garden teeming with supernatural darkness, seemed to solidify around us. It was as if the universe itself was holding its breath, waiting for our next move.

"We don't have a choice, do we?" Grant finally spoke, resignation lining his hoarse voice.

"No, we don't," I confirmed, my eyes meeting Donald's as he continued his incantations. "But we do have a chance. A slim one, perhaps, but a chance nonetheless."

As the last word left my lips, something extraordinary happened.

The necklace and pendant, which had been eerily still since our descent into this nightmarish reality, began to glow. The light emanating from them was not of this world; it was both comforting and unsettling, as if they were fueled by the very energies that tethered us to this perilous threshold between worlds.

I watched as Grant, his face a mask of grief and resolve, reached for the glowing artifacts. For a moment, the world seemed to freeze around us. It was as if time itself had paused, giving us this one pivotal instant to alter the course of our fates.

Clutching the necklace and pendant tightly in his shaking hand, Grant walked over to Virginia. A guttural whisper erupted from the members of the Midnight Veil, their eyes glowing an unholy red, yet they made no move to stop him.

Standing over Virginia's lifeless form, he held the glowing necklace close to her, his eyes shutting tightly as if trying to will her back to life with every fiber of his being. A tear slid down his cheek, landing on the necklace, which pulsed even brighter for a split second.

Then, the unthinkable happened.

The whispering of the Midnight Veil cult ceased. A sudden, penetrating silence fell over the garden, broken only by the soft, almost inaudible sobs from Grant. It was as if the world itself were holding its breath, waiting for what would come next.

The necklace and pendant continued to glow, but Virginia remained still—lifeless.

Grant's shoulders sagged in defeat, the weight of his hopes and dreams crumbling before him. But just as he was about to withdraw the necklace, something extraordinary occurred.

The ground beneath us trembled, the air around us pulsing with a newfound energy. And then, to our collective shock, the portal—the wretched doorway that had led us to this infernal brink—began to waver, as if becoming less certain, less fixed in the fabric of reality.

Grant looked at the necklace, then back at Virginia, and then at each of us, his eyes widening with a mixture of disbelief and a glimmer of hope. But before he could say anything, a voice broke the silence—a voice that was neither of this world, nor the next, a voice filled with a malevolence that shook us to our very core.

"Do you really think you can stop what's coming?" the voice sneered, emanating from the shadows that surrounded the portal. "She is just the beginning."

And then, with a scream that will haunt me for the rest of my life, the ground opened up beneath Virginia's body, swallowing her into the abyss.

I was helpless to save her.

I had failed her once again and for one last time.

Chapter Nineteen—Grant

My eyes were still red, my cheeks wet with the tears I'd shed over Virginia's lifeless body, when a new figure emerged from the flickering portal. The light from the unstable gateway cast eerie shadows over his face, but there was something hauntingly familiar about him.

Although I could not recall seeing him before, everything about him was familiar to me. He looked to be between Alan and Pettie's ages. He was a young boy, but his eyes carried the weight of something older, something heavy.

He walked straight toward me, a phantom guided by an invisible compass. He reached for me—no, he reached for the now glowing necklace that dangled from my neck. My heart thundered in my chest, as if it recognized a melody from a song long forgotten.

It was the strangest sensation, like staring into a mirror that reflected a past life.

The air was thick with tension, a mixture of dread and awe, like the moment right before a storm breaks. I felt everyone's eyes on me, their gazes filled with questions I couldn't answer.

Still hovering my hand over the necklace, the garden became cold as ice. Evelyn's shout shattered the silence like a dropped glass.

"Don't give it to him, Grant! Step away!"

Her voice was soaked in desperation, a frantic edge cutting through the heavy air. My eyes met hers; I saw genuine fear there. It was as if the ground beneath me shifted, and for a moment, I hesitated. Her words were like a splash of cold water, jolting me out of whatever trance I had fallen into.

The boy still stood before me, his outstretched hand now seeming less like a gesture of familiarity and more like a snare. But his eyes...those eyes pulled at a memory buried so deep I'd nearly forgotten it existed.

"Grant?" Evelyn asked cautiously. "Come back to us."

The tension thickened, each second stretching out, as if time itself held its breath, waiting for my next move. Evelyn's words echoed in my mind, conflicting with the emotion welling up inside me.

I felt a rush of emotions as the boy's face slowly came into focus, each feature triggering a cascade of long-buried memories. And then, as he smiled, something inside me broke. Tears filled my eyes and spilled down my cheeks, each drop carrying with it years of forgotten sorrow and lost time.

The boy's smile seemed to say, "You remember now, don't you?" And I did.

Isaiah Sullivan. My brother, my twin.

I remembered a shared laughter, a twin bed, matching outfits, and then an empty space where he used to be—a void that had long gone unacknowledged, a chapter of my life sealed away.

Quincy! Why didn't you remind me?

As tears blurred my vision, I felt as if the ground beneath me was crumbling, not out of fear, but from the sheer emotional weight of the moment.

The son I'd saved, the daughter I'd almost lost, and now the brother who'd been taken from me; it was all converging, a whirlwind of past and present, of love and loss. And Virginia, my lovely wife...

And so, as he stepped closer, that smile still lighting up his face, I wept freely. For the first time in many years, I felt a sense of wholeness, as if a part of me that had been amputated had miraculously grown back.

For a moment, all the years fell away, and I was a young boy again, holding my twin brother Isaiah's hand as we explored the world together. But that world had torn us apart, a rupture in the fabric of our family that had never mended. He had vanished, simply disappeared one sunny afternoon in the very garden where I now stood. It was a wound that had never healed, driving our mother to the edge of madness and leaving a rift in our family that even time couldn't bridge.

"Isaiah," I whispered, my voice breaking with the name that I had long avoided even in the privacy of my own thoughts.

He nodded, that serene smile still gracing his face as though to say, "It's me, Grant. I've been waiting for you to return."

The realization that I was facing my long-lost brother, the other half of me, felt like an anchor had been lifted from my soul. And yet, with that lifting came a new heaviness, the weight of years lost and the ramifications of what his disappearance had done to our family.

Evelyn, Donald, Pettie, and Alan watched in astonishment, bearing witness to a reunion that defied the realms of possibility. But none of that mattered now. For the first time, I was seeing my life in its entirety, the joy and the pain, the love and the loss. And at the center of it was Isaiah, offering me the chance for redemption or damnation.

My mind swirled with memories, ones that I had tucked away so deeply that they'd become nearly mythical in nature.

My mother's voice echoed in my head, a litany of sobs and prayers. "He's gone, he's gone, oh my Isaiah is gone," she had wailed, her sanity unraveling thread by thread until she became a husk of the woman she once was.

The memories played out like a film reel, one moment projecting the vibrant laughter of two young boys playing in the garden, the next capturing the inconsolable anguish of a mother who had lost one of her sons to an unexplainable tragedy. I had lived my life under the shadow of Isaiah's disappearance, a mystery that had never been solved and had instead festered into a painful family secret. Somehow, I'd put him out of my mind. I'd put everything out of my mind except my education and later my ill-fated career.

The weight of those years pressed down on me as I looked into Isaiah's eyes, seeing both the brother I had lost and the symbol of all the pain that had followed. My chest tightened, a knot of complex emotions that included regret, guilt, and a sadness so profound it felt like it could swallow me whole.

"I'm so sorry," I managed to say, my voice laden with the weight of decades of unspoken feelings. "So sorry for everything."

Isaiah extended his arm, his hand open in invitation. It was as though time itself had stilled, the air thick with expectation and palpable tension. My heart thrummed in my chest, a cacophony of beats that felt like they could be a coded message from the universe, urging me to make a decision that could change the fate of everyone involved.

My fingers trembled as they touched the cool metal of the necklace. The pendant seemed to pulse with a hidden power, as if it recognized the gravity of this moment.

My eyes met Evelyn's, and I saw a mixture of terror and hope in her gaze. Donald had a stern look on his face, fraught with worry, but also tinged with anticipation. Pettie and Alan, my children who had endured so much, seemed to hover between two worlds, both afraid and hopeful, their young faces a canvas of innocence and hard-won wisdom.

My hand moved almost of its own accord, a magnetic pull guiding it towards Isaiah's open palm. The instant our hands met, an electric charge surged through me, like lightning forking through a tempestuous sky. It felt as though the very fabric of reality trembled, ready to either mend itself or tear apart even further.

My voice quivered as I whispered, "Take it. Please, make this right."

Isaiah's eyes, so like my own, met mine with a gentle, loving smile. "Thank you, brother," he said, his voice imbued with a timeless wisdom that seemed to transcend his young age.

And then he grasped the necklace, his hand closing around the pendant that had come to symbolize so much pain and hope, regret and possibility.

Isaiah's fingers wrapped around the necklace, and as they did, a light emanated from the pendant, bathing us all in its soft, ethereal glow. A feeling of deep tranquility, like the first rays of dawn breaking the dark of night, washed over me.

"I love you, Grant," Isaiah murmured, his voice tinged with a haunting sweetness that resonated in the depths of my soul.

"I love you too, Isaiah," I replied, my voice catching in my throat as tears blurred my vision. It was a moment of heartbreaking beauty, the final note in a symphony of human emotions that had played out in this surreal garden.

With a serene smile, my brother stepped back, still holding the necklace high above his head. As he moved, his form began to blur and shift, as though he were made of stardust, ready to return to the cosmos.

Everyone—Evelyn, Donald, Alan, and Pettie—watched in a mixture of awe and trepidation. What was about to happen? Would this end our nightmare, or plunge us deeper into chaos?

Isaiah turned and walked towards the swirling vortex of the portal, his silhouette framed by the uncanny blue light that seemed to dance and flicker like the flames of some otherworldly fire.

And then he stepped into it.

The moment Isaiah stepped into the portal, holding the necklace aloft, an explosion of sound and light erupted from the vortex. It was as if the universe itself had cracked open, releasing a force beyond mortal understanding.

We all threw ourselves to the ground, instinctively seeking cover from the unknown. My heart was pounding in my chest, each beat a drumroll in the soundtrack of our collective fear and hope.

I dared to look up just in time to see the members of the Midnight Veil, who had been whispering their malevolent incantations, now screaming in terror and confusion. They seemed disoriented, their eyes wide with a fear that mirrored my own, but for entirely different reasons.

Then the unbelievable happened.

The necklace began to glow brighter and brighter, its light expanding in a radiant burst that enveloped everything—us, the cult, the garden, even the portal. And the cult members, they started to disintegrate, their forms dissolving into particles that were pulled towards the necklace like iron to a magnet.

Their screams became a cacophonous wail that filled the air, a symphony of despair that heralded their own undoing. They fought, they resisted, but one by one, they were drawn into the glowing pendant of the necklace.

And then, as quickly as it had all started, it was over. The light receded, the screams fell silent, and the necklace seemed to absorb the last remnants of the Midnight Veil.

Isaiah turned back to look at me, his eyes gleaming with an ethereal light. The necklace and pendant, still glowing, seemed to pulse in his hands, as if they were a beating heart. With a nod and a smile that I'll carry with me to the end of my days, he stepped into the azure light of the portal.

The light surged one final time, its luminance reaching an almost blinding intensity, and then—like a candle abruptly snuffed out—it vanished. The portal was gone. The necklace was gone. Isaiah was gone.

My heart was an odd mixture of elation and sorrow. We had won; the Midnight Veil was no more, and the terrible portal was sealed. But in that victory, I lost my brother all over again.

The garden was still, the day returned to normal, if normal could ever describe what life would be from this point on. I looked at Evelyn, Donald, Alan, and Pettie. Their faces were etched with a combination of relief, exhaustion, and a newfound resolve. We had faced the abyss, and we had come out the other side, scarred, but alive.

But even as we breathed our collective sigh of relief, I felt a weight lift from me, yet settle within me at the same time.

Isaiah had given us this victory, but at the cost of unearthing old wounds, old memories.

I was whole, yet forever changed.

Epilogue—Evelyn

The air was heavy with sorrow as we laid Virginia to rest in a secluded, sun-dappled grove, a stark contrast to the ominous atmosphere of Laurel House. The trees whispered their ancient lullabies, their leaves rustling as if paying respects to the departed. This place was imbued with a natural serenity, a final refuge we hoped would offer Virginia the peace she deserved.

Pettie's eyes were red-rimmed, her face a canvas of grief and confusion, as if each tear that slid down her cheek posed a question she couldn't articulate. Alan stood next to her, his young shoulders hunched under an invisible weight, his eyes empty chasms that reflected the world-altering loss we all felt.

How could two children adapt to a world that had shifted so inexplicably, so cruelly?

Donald and I stood beside them like twin pillars, our presence meant to serve as a sanctuary, however feeble, against the storm of emotions battering them. My heart felt like it was brimming over, filled with a mixture of sorrow, sympathy, and a nebulous form of hope. Hope that in time, the wounds would heal even if the scars remained, a testament to battles fought and loved ones lost.

We were all drifting on an emotional sea, each of us an island of pain and bewilderment. Yet standing there, in that tranquil grove, it was as if the universe had paused for a moment to mourn with us. Virginia was gone, but in that instant, she felt closer than ever—as if her spirit had infused the air, the trees, the very soil we had laid her in.

Grant stood a short distance away, his silhouette etched against the lingering light of the setting sun. He gazed down at the freshly turned earth, his posture a blend of stoicism and fragility, as if he were a statue carved from both marble and glass.

His eyes, windows to a soul deeply marked by love and loss, held an unfathomable depth. It was as if he were trying to communicate with Virginia beyond the veil of mortality, seeking some divine acknowledgment that his love for her would continue, transcendent of life and death.

As the rest of us stood in our quiet circles of grief, I heard him whisper, his voice almost drowned out by the evening wind, but resonating with an emotional frequency that carried across the space between us.

"I promise to keep them safe, my love. That's my vow to you, for all eternity."

His words were drenched in sorrow, yes, but they also reverberated with a spine-tingling resolve. It was as if, in that moment, he'd forged a covenant not just with the memory of Virginia, but with the very fibers of the universe.

His promise was a tangible thing, as real as the earth upon which he stood, as inescapable as the setting sun that marked the end of one chapter and the inevitable dawn of another.

There was a sacredness to his vow, an unspoken bond that melded his soul with Virginia's in a celestial union that would hold firm, whether in this world, or the next. And it struck me that his promise was not just for Virginia, but for all of us—his love and resolve, a fortress against the darkness we had all witnessed, a beacon guiding us toward a future where hope might, once again, find its foothold.

The air was thick with a sense of finality as we collectively came to a resolution: Laurel House and Bryan Bay were now chapters in our pasts, sealed and set aside like ancient tomes teeming with lessons both harrowing and enlightening. We could no longer dwell in those shadows, in a place where every corner might hold a whisper of the malevolent energies we had fought so hard to escape.

Donald and I had long since relocated our lives and work to a more secluded, tranquil corner of Florida—a sanctuary of sorts, awash in the healing embrace of sun and sea. It was a place far removed from the haunting memories and dark entanglements that had ensnared us for so long.

The aura there was different, as if the very air exhaled sighs of relief, and the waters held no reflections of lurking evils.

Now, the Sullivan family, irrevocably changed and in desperate need of a fresh start, would join us. Their eyes, once windows to simple joys and everyday concerns, were now like deep wells, filled with an understanding of mysteries most people are fortunate never to face.

We would stand together in our new sanctuary, an alliance forged through shared trials and the kind of existential struggles that either break you or build you into something stronger.

This new chapter felt like a second chance, a blank page upon which we could inscribe a narrative untainted by the malevolence that had so cruelly invaded our lives. And yet, there was also the unspoken acknowledgment among us that the past was now a part of us, indelible as ink, its lessons etched into the marrow of our bones.

It was a bittersweet symphony of sorts; we were like refugees who had survived a storm and found ourselves on new shores, forever marked, but still standing.

The weight of our experiences had become a part of our essence, and as we moved forward, it was with the wisdom that only comes from surviving the unimaginable.

The atmosphere inside the carriage grew dense, like we were driving through a thick fog of foreboding that had nothing to do with the weather. The organ music still echoed in my ears, its haunting melody a soundtrack to the unease settling deep in my bones.

It emanated from the old stone church, its steeple piercing the sky as if reaching for an absent grace. The sound seemed to float, disembodied, through the empty streets, imbuing the very air with a sense of spectral melancholy.

The town felt like a desolate ghost itself, a place devoid of life, yet brimming with memories that clung to its architecture like cobwebs. As we drove through, not a single resident appeared—no farewell waves, no lingering glances. It was as though we had become phantoms in a landscape of forgotten souls, the town's silence serving as our only adieu.

Just when I felt the knot of tension slightly loosen, as if we were finally distancing ourselves from a nightmarish tale, the sudden jingle of Donald's pocket watch broke the stillness. The sound seemed disproportionately loud, shattering the fragile peace like a stone through glass. He pulled out a small, folded piece of parchment from his coat pocket, and I saw his face lose color, as if drained by some spectral hand. "It's a message," he said, handing me the note with a trembling hand. "How in the world?"

The words written in elegant but hurried script seemed to sear itself into my eyes: "The Veil may be torn, but the tapestry is far from unraveled."

My heart skipped a beat, not in exhilaration but in trepidation. We were driving away, yes, but were we truly leaving anything behind?

For in that chilling moment, I realized our fight might be won, but the war was far from over.

The spider was still out there, unseen but ever-present, spinning new webs in the cavernous darkness, awaiting its next opportunity to strike.

I shivered in the sunlight. I pressed my lips together and snatched the note from Donald. Crumpling it up, I tossed it out of the open carriage window.

I watched it blow away, along with Pettie who practically sat in my lap day and night. I didn't mind at all. I kissed the top of her head and tidied her bow.

"Don't look back, Pettie. Never look back."

"Yes, Aunt Evelyn. Never look back."

I pulled Pettie higher in my lap and I closed my eyes. Let this end. Let this all come to an end. The sooner we would have a new beginning.

I'll make sure they're okay, Virginia. I promise.

I didn't hear her voice but heard the faint rustling of skirts. Her skirts. I knew it was her, with us one moment and then gone the next.

That would be enough.

Rest in peace, Virginia. Don't wake up, sister.

Author's Note

Dear Readers,

First and foremost, thank you for journeying with me into the dark and intricate world of "Whispers." This tale—full of love, loss, and haunting mysteries—has been a journey for me as much as I hope it has been for you.

The inspiration for "Whispers" came from a blend of personal experiences, extensive research, and the rich tapestry of folklore that surrounds the supernatural. While the events and characters in this book are entirely fictional, they touch on the fears, hopes, and uncertainties that we all encounter at some point in our lives.

The town of Bryan Bay, the enigmatic Laurel House, and the malevolent entities of the Midnight Veil were constructed from the cobwebs of my imagination. However, the emotional undertones were harvested from the real human experiences of love, loss, and the quest for redemption and closure.

I must extend my heartfelt thanks to everyone who contributed to the making of this book. My editor, my family, and of course, you—the readers. Without your continued support and eagerness to walk beside me into the realms of the unknown, "Whispers" would remain an untold story.

As you close this book, remember that the world of "Whispers" lives on, lurking in the shadows, always waiting for the right moment to ensnare the curious. Keep your eyes open for upcoming stories in this universe; we've only just scratched the surface.

Once again, thank you for allowing me to share this world with you. Until we meet again, keep the whispers at bay.

All my best,

M. L. Bullock

Don't miss out!

Visit the website below and you can sign up to receive emails whenever M.L. Bullock publishes a new book. There's no charge and no obligation.

https://books2read.com/r/B-A-CXMC-OHLQC

BOOKS 2 READ

Connecting independent readers to independent writers.

Also by M.L. Bullock

Create and Prosper
The Prolific Writer: How to Write and Create a Successful Catalog of Books

Desert Queen Saga
The Tale of Nefret
The Falcon Rises
The Kingdom of Nefertiti
The Song of the Bee Eater

Devecheaux Antiques and Haunted Things Trilogy Series
A Cup of Shadows
A Voice From Her Past
A Watch Of Weeping Angels

Gulf Coast Paranormal
The Ghosts of Kali Oka Road
The Ghosts of the Crescent Theater

A Haunting on Bloodgood Row
The Legend of the Ghost Queen
A Haunting at Dixie House
The Ghost Lights of Forrest Field
The Ghost of Gabrielle Bonet
The Ghost of Harrington Farm
The Creature on Crenshaw Road
A Ghostly Ride in Gulfport
The Ghosts of Phoenix No.7
The Maelstrom of the Leaf Academy
The Ghosts of Oakleigh House
The Spirits of Brady Hall
The Gray Lady of Wilmer

Gulf Coast Paranormal Extra
Horror Ever After

Gulf Coast Paranormal Season Two
The Wayland Manor Haunting
The Beast of Limerick House
The Beast of Limerick House
A Haunting at Goliath Cave
Death Among the Roses
The Captain of Water Street
Return to the Leaf Academy

Gulf Coast Paranormal Trilogy Series
Ghosted

Haunted
Dead
Spooked
Paranormal

Haunting Passions
For the Love of Shadows
Her Haunted Heart

Idlewood
The Ghosts of Idlewood
Dreams of Idlewood
The Whispering Saint
The Haunted Child

Laurel House
Whispers

Lost Camelot
Guinevere Unconquered
The Undead Queen of Camelot

Lost Camelot Trilogy
Guinevere Forever

Marietta
The Bones of Marietta
Footsteps of Angels

Morgans Rock
The Haunting of Joanna Storm
The Hall of Shadows
The Ghost of Joanna Storm

Return to Seven Sisters
The Roses of Mobile
All the Summer Roses
Blooms Torn Asunder
A Garden of Thorns
Wreath of Roses

Scary Fall Stories
Horrible Little Things

Seven Sisters
Seven Sisters
Moonlight Falls On Seven Sisters
Shadows Stir At Seven Sisters
The Stars That Fell

The Stars We Walked Upon
The Sun Rises Over Seven Sisters
Beyond Seven Sister
Ghost on a Swing

Shabby Hearts
A Touch Of Shabby
Shabbier By The Minute
Shabby By Night
Shabby All The Way
Star Spangled Shabby

Southern Gothic
Being With Beau
Death's Last Darling
Spook House

Sugar Hill
Wife Of The Left Hand
Fire On The Ramparts
Blood By Candlelight
The Starlight Ball
His Lovely Garden

Summerleigh
The Belles of Desire, Mississippi

The Ghost Of Jeoprady Belle
The Lady In White
Loxley Belle

Supernatural Support Group
Circle of Shadows

The Mummy Queen's Revenge
Queen Mummy

Twelve to Midnight
Mary Twelves

Standalone
Christmas at Seven Sisters
The Hauntings of Idlewood
Lost Camelot
The Desert Queen Collection
Haunting Passions
Ghosts on a Plane
Halloween Screams
Dead Is the Loneliest Place to Be
River Run

About the Author

Author M.L. Bullock enjoys the laid-back atmosphere and the spooky vibe of the Gulf Coast, especially the region's historic districts and sites. When she isn't visiting her favorite haunts in New Orleans or Old Mobile, you can find her flipping through old photographs or newspaper clippings in search of new inspiration.

Read more at www.mlbullock.com.